A Cold Wind Blowing

Books by Barbara Willard

THE SUMMER WITH SPIKE

HETTY

THE HOUSE WITH ROOTS

THE BATTLE OF WEDNESDAY WEEK

THREE AND ONE TO CARRY

CHARITY AT HOME

THE RICHLEIGHS OF TANTAMOUNT

THE GROVE OF GREEN HOLLY

THE FAMILY TOWER

THE TOPPLING TOWERS

The Forest Novels

THE LARK AND THE LAUREL

THE SPRIG OF BROOM

A COLD WIND BLOWING

Local History Series

CHICHESTER AND LEWES

Barbara Willard

A Cold Wind Blowing

Longman

LONGMAN GROUP LIMITED LONDON
Associated companies, branches and representatives
throughout the world

First published 1972

ISBN 0 582 15855 9

Printed in Great Britain
by Ebenezer Baylis and Son Limited
The Trinity Press, Worcester, and London

Contents

Contents

1

The Three Brothers

His father's news, rather anxiously given, had delighted Piers Medley. He was still smiling as he went out of the house. Only as he reached the big stable block and crossed its paved yard did he remember that though he and young Richard would both be overjoyed, Harry, the eldest of the three brothers, might not be so pleased. Hurrying out into the April weather in search of the other two, Piers could see that Harry might have cause to complain, that he would complain, and that it would be difficult to deal patiently with his particular response to the tidings.

Two grooms rode in from exercising young stock—two horses ridden, two led—and Piers shouted across 'Have you seen my brothers?'

'I see Master Richard run down along by the river, sir,' one lad called back.

'Where there's one brother there'll be two, mostlike,' Piers said. He stood to watch the riders. 'How's Verity go, Tom?'

'Keen, sir. A bit heggling to hold in, to speak true.'

'No sign of the lameness, then?'

'Hem-a-bit, Master Piers. She go proud.'

'Dignity look fit, too,' Piers said, to the second boy. 'Keep her to it, Adam.'

'I shall, sir,' Adam answered.

'Get 'em in and rubbed down, then. Sun's warm enough but there's still a smell of frost.'

Piers nodded to the lads and left them grinning, pleased with themselves and pleased with him. He strode on down the sloping land to the high pale that kept out the deer, and went through the bottom gate. He was immediately among trees, birch just shaking into leaf, the green so tender it was almost gold. This seedling growth, only a few years old, was a fringe round the Ghylls Hatch land on its southern boundary, and some would fall next autumn when the deer fence was renewed; the boundary was pushed out slyly year by year, stealing the forest foot by foot. The ground beneath the young trees shone with primroses, the enormous spread of bloom so quilted and billowy that the over-ripe violets and tattered wind flowers that had come first were neatly covered. Piers followed a coney track through the birches and emerged on the high bank above the river. It was not much more than a stream, but all waterways hereabouts were called rivers and Piers would not have thought to use any more modest term. He stood quietly, looking about him and listening.

First he heard the bird noise that was all about him and above him, then the singing of the water in a different key. Then he heard voices—Harry's down in his boot-bottoms, where it had settled about seven years ago when he touched fifteen, and then the high excited chattering of young Richard. There was an echo about here that took both high and low and tossed them from side to side.

'Catch him! Catch him!' Richard cried. 'Catch him, do, Harry—or I'll catch him! Bring him home to cook!'

A growl from Harry told Piers that he was reproving their young brother. The brown trout in these waters were tasty and sweet, but Harry would be mighty stern about when and how to take them.

'Harry! Richard!' Piers shouted, and his voice in its turn went bouncing along the coombe.

Harry shouted back, and almost instantly Richard burst up the bank from the river and dashed at Piers, and greeted him with wild pummelling and butting. Piers swung him up and tucked him under one arm, head down and bare heels beating. Richard twisted and lashed like any fish beached and gasping.

'Take me to Harry, minnow,' Piers commanded.

He set Richard on his feet and gave him a shove in the small of his bony young back. There was all of eight years between them, but Piers was always content to give time to the ten-year-old. They were like two halves of an apple, their father had once said, the bigger shedding some size to match the smaller, the smaller gaining from the generosity of the larger, so that, mysteriously, they matched.

Harry had been cutting withies as well as instructing Richard in fish lore. The longest was taller than he was, pliant and whippy, and he might use it as a rod when it was ready. The rest could go for basket making and keep the maids busy in next winter's long days.

'A good afternoon,' said Harry, without turning to look at Piers; he stated a fact that was also a greeting. Harry was not always over-free with his words, hoarding them, as it often seemed, for future occasions when he might feel a real need.

'And a good afternoon to you, brother,' said Piers.

Something studied in his tone made Harry pause and look round. 'What's took you?' he asked.

'I came a-purpose to bring you news. But if you're too busy to hear 'em . . .'

'Private news, brother?'

'For the present.'

'Get you off home, Dickory,' Harry commanded. 'Leave your elders talk alone.'

'Nay, Harry—I'll keep mum,' the boy wheedled. 'As a mouse, I will. I'll close my ears up, come you wish it.'

'There's no good reason he shouldn't stay, Harry. It's family-private—for the present.'

'Spit it out, then, for Heaven's sweet sake,' said Harry, and he looked a shade uneasy. 'Death or sickness, is it? War, is it? Or more rebellion?'

'I may as well come out straight with it. Our father's taking a new wife.'

Harry stared and did not answer. The expression went out of his face, leaving it blank and stony.

'Ten year a widower, Harry,' Piers said gently. 'Best remember that.'

'Who?'

'You look fearsome thundery, brother?'

'*Who is it?*'

'This is good news, surelye. What d'you say, Dickory? Good, isn't it?'

'Judith!' cried Richard, 'Oh it must be Judith!'

'Who else? Who else, minnow? Did I scare you?'

'You did scare me,' Richard admitted, nodding till his dark hair fell in his eyes. He swallowed and then began to grin.

'You take it pretty cool, Piers,' Harry said. 'Seems our mother's quite forgot.'

'That's a false lie, Harry Medley. She never shall be— nor the day she die—my birthday, eight-year-old. No, nor how she left new Richard wailing behind . . . And let you recall, brother, how Judith took him to nurse because she'd lost her own. He'd have died for sure, poor minnow, wi'out Judith had milk wasting.' He put his arm round Richard and hugged the boy against his side. 'I know what we owe Judith.'

'She make my father very comfortable the last years.'

'She make all of us comfortable, Harry.'

'You know well what I mean. She warm his bed for him.'

'Then high time they were decently wed, Harry Medley. Shame on you for thinking less.' He laughed at Harry's black expression that looked very ill on his fair complexion, the colouring both he and Piers had inherited from their mother. 'Come, Harry—say God bless 'em.'

'You've forgot something,' Harry said.

'No,' Piers said, soberly enough. 'I've forgot nothing.'

At Christmas last, Harry had been betrothed to Anne Furnival. Her father was an impoverished baronet with a small manor ten or twelve miles east of Ghylls Hatch, almost into Kent, whose fortunes had veered with his political sympathies. They were now at their lowest on account of fines and confiscations resulting from his loud championing of King Henry's first queen, Katherine. He had been unable to offer much of a dowry. The bargain was levelled by the fact that Harry, though his mother had been well born, could offer no pedigree on the paternal side—the origins of Master Medley of Ghylls Hatch were accepted as being obscure.

'Anne was to be mistress at Ghylls Hatch,' Harry said.

'You know how kind and comfortable Judith is—how modest. She will welcome your Anne and let her have her way about the house.'

'But Judith'll be Dame Medley, and Anne only Mistress Harry. That's not what her father was promised.'

'Anne's sixteen year old,' said Piers, beginning to get heated. 'Is Judith to be ordered by a girl?'

'Come to that—is Anne to be ordered by a woman who was born into service at Mantlemass? Judith was niece to our mother's old nurse Meg—you know that, much as I do.'

'And our father know it, and can see how Judith might be put down by Anne! He'll not abide that, and rightly. Nor could I, nor Richard here. And you should not be able to abide it, brother. That'd be a wicked cruel thing after all she done for us.'

'Well, I'm not so wise and all-loving and Godly Christian as you!' cried Harry. 'I say the contract's broke by this. I'll lose Anne when her father hears!'

'Never believe it!'

'We saw the big trout, Piers—didn't we, Harry?' said Richard nervously, hoping to distract his brothers from their wrangle.

'To hell with that!' Harry shouted. 'I've more important things to think on. Hold your tongue, you silly brat!'

He turned away sharply, kicking aside the withies that he had gathered into a heap and blundering away from the other two up the bank and quickly out of sight. He was all but crying.

Richard looked anxiously at Piers, and Piers smiled to encourage him. Richard put down his shoulders that had hunched at Harry's distress. He was the merest hint crooked in his spine and carried one shoulder a fraction higher than the other. There was not much in it, certainly, but when he was disturbed he brought the straight shoulder up to meet the other in a defensive manner—rather as a mouse will round its back and wait, listening and smelling for danger. A boy in Staglye village, who had a truly misshapen back, was not only jeered at by his fellows but was despised, so they said, by his own mother. No one had ever seen fit to mock Richard, but he did lack a little strength because of it. Once he had stood stamping and crying with bitter rage because he could not haul himself up on to the back of the tallest mount at Ghylls Hatch. His father had lifted him into the saddle, checking him as he prepared to ride off, holding the bridle with one hand and Richard's ankle with the other. 'Wear it as a badge, Dickory,' he had said. 'Such things come by inheritance—as much as armorial bearings.' Richard had no idea, then or since, what his father meant. All the same, after that he did not allow himself to be troubled by his slight infirmity . . .

Piers was gathering up the withies that Harry had scattered. Richard loved both his brothers, but Piers he loved so deeply that he was sure he would lie down and die for him if need be, would stand terrible torture if it should save him from disaster, and starve to give him a crust. Piers was slightly built, not very tall—but steely, Richard always thought. Because he himself was dark and curly, Richard admired all the more his brother's thick straight fair hair, his skin that was fair without being pink and browned smoothly in summer time. Piers was a better rider than any at Ghylls Hatch— better than their father, even. Master Medley insisted that this was simply because he himself was getting on in life. At Piers's age, he had boasted to make them laugh, he could have ridden a winged dragon with ease.

'What do you say, Richard?' Piers was asking as he collected the willow cuttings. 'Shall you be happy to call our dear Judith *mother*?'

Richard was silent a moment, wondering how much to admit. When he and Judith were together, the two of them, he called her Mother anyway. In fact there was even more to it than that, which he had never spoken of and could not have spoken of now if Harry had still been there.

'I thought she *was* my mother, Piers. I thought it till I was near seven year old.'

'Were you sad to find the truth?'

'I were sore distressed. True enough, I were all but despairing, brother—which is a sin,' said Richard, shaking his head to recall the sense of shock and loss when he learnt that Judith was only his foster mother. 'Piers—are you laughing?'

'God forbid. I can well understand what you felt.'

'But I should love my own mother, seems to me,' said Richard, looking worried.

'There's no man living can truly love what he never knew. Judith truly has been your mother—in all but bearing you. There was two babes born—you know that already—and one died and one mother died. Only they did not belong together.' Piers sighed and shook his head, for he never could quite accept the cruelty of it. 'Strange that may seem, minnow, but so we know God willed it.'

It made Richard uneasy to think of his dead mother— he was sure he should be unhappy without her but life went easily enough for him with Judith to love, his father to admire almost as a god, his two brothers to watch him and shove him the way they felt he should go—which had so far always been the way he wanted. His mother for sure was safe in heaven, and Judith's innocent infant must be with her, for Judith had often said so. The two women, then, had simply exchanged babies, Richard decided; and he sought about for some good reason for this, aside from the will of God.

'Could be she looked for a daughter, Piers. That make sense to me. If not, for sure she'd have taken me with her.'

'Surelye, she was heartily sick of nothing but great lads about her,' Piers agreed. 'Us, and the three more that died—the first Richard, and Lewis and Edmund. Lord—think hard how it might be if there were six of us at Ghylls Hatch now!'

'And what should I be called?' cried Richard, who had not thought of this before. 'I could not be Richard Medley the Second!'

'Still, I'd not have despised a sister, Dickory. Brave and clever, my father say of the women of our family. Think how our grandmother rule over Mantlemass— she's no timmersome widow. And there was her aunt, old Dame Elizabeth—as firm and sure in business, they say, as any man, and better than many.'

'But my Mantlemass cousins, now,' said Richard. 'Ask me, brother, that's a sad and sickly lot of women growing up there now.'

He blushed when Piers spluttered into laughter. Their uncle Simon Mallory's three daughters were prim as daisies and meek as does, but Richard's old-gentlemanly comment seemed supremely funny to the older boy. After a second, Richard grinned. Piers must be allowed his laugh. He was at his best with young things. He was most skilled of any at Ghylls Hatch in handling the mares when they foaled, the foals if they were orphaned. It had been so ever since he was nine years old and stayed all night in the straw with a sickly foal whose dam had died, suckling the little creature with rags dipped in goat's milk, that everyone said would kill it. The foal lived, and now, graceful if never robust, she carried Piers about the forest. All that had happened less than a year after his own mother died, so perhaps he had felt a special kinship with the orphan. There remained a great bond between them, for Sola, as he had named her, let no other rider near her, stepping back delicately and shaking her ears even if it was only Richard who approached . . .

By now Piers had collected all the cuttings that Harry had scattered in his rage. 'Come on home now,' he said to Richard. 'Here—you carry the short stammers and I'll take the long.'

Richard accepted the load with pleasure, grateful for the talk, even if it ended in being laughed at, for Piers had treated him as an equal in confidence.

'Will they have a feast, think you?' he asked his brother, as they scrambled up the steep bank. 'Father, I mean, and Judith. A marriage feast?'

'I'd say not. I'd say they'd do all quiet and ordinary. Maybe our uncle will marry them. It's my guess they'll spare the feast to Harry and Anne Furnival.'

'There's a mort of marrying to be seen to,' said Richard, shaking his head. 'Don't you go marrying, Piers. I'll have to stay as I be years and years before it come to my turn. I'd be left alone, come you took a wife.'

'I won't,' said Piers. 'Anyways on—not till I find the

Queen of Fairyland—and that'd be a fine long hunt.'

Richard smiled, for in his heart he did not think it impossible that Piers, if he wanted a bride, should fail to find some marvel.

'Now you listen, minnow,' Piers said, when they were in sight of home. 'Don't you go nabbling about the house and telling all of what's to pass. The servants shall know in due time. Hear me?'

'Aye, Piers. And I give my word. But mayn't I tell Judith?'

'That she and our father are to wed? She'll know that of herself, I trust!'

They were crossing the wide open land that lay to the south-westward of Ghylls Hatch. The business and occupation of the place was fully displayed ahead of them. The pastures were full of horses—riding horses, draught beasts, and those deep-chested weight-carriers that were bred to bear men in armour, to war or to joust. The quiet spring sky over all was tinged with the delicate green promise of a late frost. As if exhausted by a day's uninterrupted shining, the sun had fuzzed wearily into the mist rising off the warmed countryside, where the remaining russet was being drained at last out of the year-old tumbled bracken. Far off, beyond the cleared track that led by Mantlemass towards the distant sea-coast, it was possible nowadays before summer came to catch a sight of the manor house itself. Much beechwood had been cut over the last years and the place had grown so greatly it was all but a hamlet. It was big enough, in fact, to warrant the church Dame Cecily Mallory had long planned to build, and they had dug out the foundations last autumn. The church was to rise, not only to the glory of God, but as a monument, a memorial to a marriage most truly made in heaven, to the memory of Dame Cecily's husband, Master Lewis Mallory of Mantlemass. He had died ten years ago, visiting London about estate business at a time of plague; it was said that fifty people in a day were dying there, and he never should have made the journey at all, only he had not been a man to shun dangers.

That had been a black year for Mantlemass and for Ghylls Hatch. It was barely six months after Master Lewis was taken that his daughter, Catherine Medley, died giving birth to Richard, her sixth son. Besides that, earlier in the year, there had been the dreadful business of Ned Springer, Judith's husband, who had been under-bailiff at Mantlemass. Master Lewis had seen his quality while he was still a boy about the farm, the son of a herdsman—he had helped and encouraged Ned and when Judith married him there were almost family festivities. Ned was a sportive sort of man, loving above all else to hunt the royal deer through the forest. There was some survey and assessment of the royal hunting grounds in progress at that time, and of all those who had poached deer with impunity year by year, Ned Springer must needs get caught. He was tried, convicted and hanged. It was not surprising that in due course his wife gave birth to a dead child.

Richard would listen for ever when Piers or Harry spoke to him of these things—how they had buried Master Lewis only three days after his return from London, on a night of mist and moonlight, and from all around for many miles neighbours and friends and tenants came through the forest bearing torches to honour him for the last time. And then how their own father, when his wife Catherine died, had shut himself up for days, and none had seen him; they left food and drink at his door but there it remained. At last Dame Cecily had come from Mantlemass. Harry and Piers and all the servants, indoor and out, the house women, the grooms, the stable boys, had followed her as she swept into the house and up the stairway to beat on the closed door.

Here Piers would pause in the telling, and Richard cry with bated breath, 'Go on! Tell what she said to him. Go on!'

'She hammered with both fists and shout out "Coward!"—and I was there, remember, and heard it. "Coward! God shall disown ye, as I will! Stand up," she cry to him, "and take what heaven sends." '

'Then the door did open . . .'

'Then the door did open,' Piers would answer without fail, 'and there he stood, and all the flesh seemed gone from his face. His shirt was tore, as if he had rent it, and his hair all in his swollen eyes . . .'

'And those eyes wild and keen as a hawk,' Richard would prompt.

'Aye—that were so—a hawk that's bated. And one said after—I misremember who—he look like his tears bin tears of blood.'

'And he said . . .? Go on, Piers.'

' "She should've bin Queen of England." '

Piers liked to end the tale there, wondering at every telling what their father could have meant, if indeed he meant anything but the raving of a man crazy with sorrow. Harry, however, was always willing to continue the tale. He went on to tell how their uncle Roger Mallory, who, as Dom Thomas, was Master of Novices at The Benedictine Priory of St Pancras, had come to Ghylls Hatch at the summons of his mother, Dame Cecily. For many hours, Harry told Richard, their father had been heard shouting blasphemies behind the closed door of the bedchamber, where Dom Thomas fought with his oldest friend's despair. At last, Dom Thomas came from the room and sent for Judith to carry in the new baby— that was Richard—whom she had taken to nurse in place of her own lost child. Then Dom Thomas, his work accomplished, rode back slowly to the Priory, exhausted, as any man is exhausted who has fought a hard battle and won . . .

'There's Harry,' Richard said, as he and Piers crossed the track towards home that spring afternoon. Harry was riding back from Mantlemass, and both his brothers knew he had rushed there to seek comfort from his

grandmother. If Dame Cecily had given any, she had
not taken long about it, for here was Harry back home
again. He kicked up his horse when he saw his brothers,
and shouted to them to wait.

'Dom Thomas is at Mantlemass,' he said when he
came up with them. 'I'm to tell our father—he's sent
for to Mantlemass. Great urgency about it.'

'What's afoot?' Piers asked.

'That I can't say, brother. But there's a 'countable lot
of deedy talk going on. We must go too, my grandmother
order me.'

'Run and find our father, Richard,' Piers said. 'I'll
get the horses, Harry.'

Richard went at once. It might take him time, for
there were plenty of places where Master Medley could
be occupied at that time of day—about his accounts
indoors, or in the stables, or far off watching some
yearling or hopeful stallion, or simply riding one of his
own good horses about his own broad acres . . . In fact,
he was crossing the hall as Richard dashed indoors, a
tallish man, strong, proud, marked still by the sadness
of a loss he had been barely strong enough to sustain and
slow to recover from; because of this, a little withdrawn
in manner—a man whose eager living had been rebuffed
by almost total despair.

'Father!' cried Richard, shouting it from the threshold.
'Piers sent me to warn you—'

'Well, gently about it,' Master Medley said. 'Warn
me, forsooth? Of what? Is the house falling down?
The horses sick and dying? Is there an enemy at the
gate?'

'Piers sent me to *tell* you,' Richard corrected himself.
'Harry was at Mantlemass, and Dom Thomas come
calling, and now Harry's sent-along home to summon
you—to Mantlemass, sir, to see Dom Thomas . . .'

'To summon me? There speaks your grandmother, I
think—not my old friend your uncle.'

'Well, there's my message,' Richard said flatly,

shrugging his shoulders because he could think of no more to add.

His father laughed, the boy sounded so old-mannish.

'My boots are on my legs, Dickory, so nothing stays me. Run and tell Piers to saddle up.'

'He done so, father.'

'Then come and wave me away up the track,' Master Medley said, putting his arm over Richard's shoulders and thrusting him towards the door.

Outside, Piers was just bringing up their father's black gelding, Dion, and leading Sola. Harry waited, still mounted and looking impatient.

'Is the summons for all Medleys, Harry?'

'Aye, sir, it is. Dom Thomas must speak to all, so he tell me.'

Once their father was mounted Harry swung away and Piers was seconds behind. The three horses whisked their fine tails and the bits jingled as they wheeled. Richard let out a shout that emerged as no more than a wail of misery.

'What now?' his father asked, checking.

'It was *all* Medleys!'

Master Medley looked down grinning at his youngest son. 'Give your hand, then.' He stooped and caught the boy by the arm and swung him up. 'You must endure sitting ahead of me. Are you too proud?'

'No, sir,' said Richard. Rather, he was proud to be seen there, for the actual physical warmth of his father's arms soothed and delighted him. Sometimes Richard knew himself so much younger than the others that he felt he barely belonged in the same generation; to share Dion's glossy back with his father restored him to an acceptable status.

Father and sons soon broke into a canter. They rode fast but easily on the well-known track. After that first glimpse of the Mantlemass chimneys, the house disappeared among trees, to emerge again, very suddenly, set before them fair and square, the farm buildings crowding about, the land secure and heartening, spreading ahead and alongside and briefly behind, where it was swallowed among fine trees.

As they clattered across the yard, a man wearing the habit of a Benedictine monk came to the door and stood waiting.

2

A Promise Given

'Ah Roger, Roger Mallory!' Master Medley cried, embracing his old friend. 'How glad I am to see you!' Then he stood back and subdued his smiles, and bent his knee, saying 'Good Dom Thomas, give an old friend your blessing.'

'I give it every day in my prayers, Medley, and well you know it. It is good to see you, too—it is many months. And the boys. Save us all—how they grow! Even young Richard is halfway to my shoulder. Indeed, he is the only boy left—the others are men.'

'They like to think so,' their father said.

'Piers, you are so like your mother. It strikes home when I see you seldom . . . Harry and I have met already today.'

'See how fast we answer your summons,' Master Medley said, still smiling in his pleasure at the meeting. Then he looked more closely at Dom Thomas. 'But you, sir—I see that all's not well with you.'

'Come indoors to the rest, Medley. There's much to

talk of. I am come from Lewes with the special com-
mendation of the Prior. Above all, to see my mother.
About the church here at Mantlemass.'

'The footings are down—and a bit more than that. You
must have seen if you rode by the usual way.'

'Yes. I did see.'

'In the spring the work can start again.'

'Come indoors.'

Piers grinned at the way Richard strode out beside his
uncle. He glanced at Harry. Harry smiled, too, but his
own worries held him fast and the smile was brief. He
went last into the house, thinking only vaguely of why
they might be there, trying to compose in his mind some
easy words with which to break the news to Anne that
she was not, after all, to be Dame Medley of Ghylls
Hatch—at least not while Judith lived. He had chosen
Anne almost three years ago, when she was still only
fourteen years old, and he had watched her at mass in the
church at Staglye. They had been aware of one another
from the moment when, head bent for the final blessing,
he had slid a glance sideways across the nave and caught
her doing the same. The mixture of piety modesty and
naughtiness in her expression had almost made him laugh
out loud, never mind where he was . . .

Dame Cecily Mallory was sitting in a fine high-backed
chair with carved arms and feet and a tapestry cushion.
Her elder son Simon was there with his solemn wife,
Mary, and their three young daughters sat in a row by the
window—Elizabeth in grey, Margaret in blue, Susannah
the youngest in a white gown rather grubby at the hem.
Susannah could never keep her feet still, and they were
kicking at the dirty hem even here at the start of what was
clearly to be a solemn family conclave. The three girls
turned their heads as if on one neck to gaze at their
cousins as they entered. Also in the room were various of
the manor servants—the secretary, the reeve, the bailiff,
and Jess Truley, who was Dame Cecily's housekeeper
and helpmeet.

'Medley,' said Dame Cecily, before even he had kissed her hand, 'we are to stop building the church.' Her voice shook slightly, not with old age, for she held herself like a girl and had usually a fine ringing voice, but with barely suppressed anger.

'Great heavens, madam,' Medley said. 'Why?'

'Roger—Dom Thomas—advises it. Because of—because of change in the air . . . But get yourself seated. And Harry and Piers. Richard, sit with your cousins, and all four keep silent and listen. And pray do not fidget,' she added, with a glance at Susannah's swinging feet.

'Susannah', her mother said, in not much more than a whisper. 'Susannah—be still.'

Richard went with some reluctance to sit by the girls, who slid eagerly along the bench to make room for him.

'Now, Roger,' Dame Cecily said to Dom Thomas, when all were settled, 'tell again what you have already told me.'

Dom Thomas sat on his mother's right hand. He had a vigorous, lively face, his hair thick and greying, curling a little around the tonsure. As he spoke his voice was full of anxiety and concern. He spoke of the troubled times, the alarms and flurries of the past few years since the King had broken with the Pope and been declared Supreme Head of the church in England.

'You all know of last autumn's revolt in the north. It failed, but it had its roots in deep dissatisfactions and fears.'

The rebellion had grown out of the religious changes, not least the sudden directive from the Crown that all monasteries and convents must be investigated, assessed, and where it seemed advisable closed down. True enough, as Dom Thomas was ready to admit, there was much anti-monastic feeling in certain parts of the country, and a lot of scandal talked. But in others the abbeys and priories had remained sources of great strength and comfort, dispensing charity, feeding the hungry and caring for the sick; and giving hospitality to travellers and pilgrims.

'Now comes terrible news from the northern counties,'
Dom Thomas said. 'A great Assize at Lincoln last
month. To try all those unpardoned and in prison since
last year's rebellion. All are condemned, and most
horribly executed—both men and women. God rest their
souls—so ends their pilgrimage of grace, as they called it.'

'They were full of courage,' Dame Cecily said.
'Misguided, maybe, but brave.'

'They have paid a dreadful penalty,' Simon Mallory
said, speaking for the first time. 'May God have mercy.'

'Amen,' said the rest, and Simon's wife, Mary, closed
her eyes and bent her head, and prayed silently.

'They did revolt against the King,' Piers said. He
cleared his throat rather nervously, for eyes that had been
lowered in respect for the victims now opened wide. His
father had swung in his seat to look at his son, and his
grandmother's eyebrows had gone up.

'So end all traitors, eh?' Dom Thomas said quietly.
'Piers, they revolted against the King's new titles—
against the threat of persecution. It was a religious revolt,
there was no politics in it.'

'Yes,' said Piers.

'Their *consciences* revolted, boy.'

'Yes, sir,' said Piers again. All he knew of the matter he
had learnt from an old schoolfellow, Robin Halacre.
Robin was at Oxford now, studying in the university.
When he was at home last Christmastide, he had said
aloud that all monasteries were corrupt and given over to
lewd practices. He had boasted, as if he would accomplish
the matter in person, that all would be closed down in
time, their inmates cast on the world, and all their great
lands and riches given elsewhere. Robin's startling
opinions, so boldly and so loudly given, had frightened
Piers as much as they had impressed him. He sat there
now in the parlour at Mantlemass, resisting his uncle's
words because Robin had seemed so great and so grand,
so daring in his youthful self-assurance—and surely
friends of an age must hang together?

'There's no treason hereabouts, uncle,' Harry said, growling it because he was always slow to speak in a crowd but had forced himself for his brother's sake. 'I never heard any man speak out against the King. There's too much else to do and think about.'

'Harry's right,' Master Medley said. 'Why, in the name of all that's sacred, should revolt in the north prevent Dame Cecily building her church at Mantlemass in the south?'

Dom Thomas shook his head. 'I should be the innocent one, friend Medley. But you've no more idea of how the world goes than a nidget.'

'I am concerned for my own affairs, surelye.'

'The monasteries here are threatened just as much as anywhere else in England. It makes no matter that all but a handful of people in these parts respect us and care for us. Did I not tell you how the King's Commissioners came to the Priory at the time of the general visitation—ferreting and enquiring? I did tell you—and more. I told you that the Prior had been indiscreet, and spoken out, and been all but accused of treason.'

'I remember. And there it rested.'

'It will not rest for ever, my friend. Not now.'

'Not now—?'

'This is what we are here to learn,' Dame Cecily said. 'My son has already explained to me why it is wise to cease building for the time being. But you must all hear. Who knows if all of us will think wisdom enough?'

'Mother, you must be guided by me,' Dom Thomas cried. 'The worst has begun, and the worst will continue. We shall not escape. We have the bitterest news of our northern brethren. Abbot Paslew of the Cistercians—at Whalley in Lancashire—is already hanged on a pretext of treason. And more are condemned on charges of sympathy with the rebels. At Bridlington, at Cartmel and Kirkstead—many are hanged and worse.'

'Mantlemass is no monastery,' Master Medley said reasonably enough. He frowned, puzzling over the realisation of change. 'We have been so quiet and undisturbed here,' he said. 'Can all this truly touch us?'

'Building a church here involves too much at a moment like this. The parish priest from Staglye will surely be the one to bless each stage of the work. And he was one of those who evaded the oath when the King was declared head of the Church.'

'He was sick,' said Harry.

'Maybe. But he'll not go unnoticed, nephew. With this connection and the other—her son a member of the chapter at St Pancras Priory . . . Well, you must see the dangers. Women have gone to the stake for lesser associations. God help us all—that is how the world goes now.'

'My aunt, Anna Jolland, my father's sister, was Superior of a small house near York,' Dame Cecily said. 'She will be long dead, for she was older than my aunt Elizabeth FitzEdmund. But I wonder how that community has fared.'

'If it is small, as you say, it will almost surely have been suppressed.'

'But the sisters would not be turned upon the world? Oh surely not! They would be so helpless.'

'There has been a choice offered, mother—to join a larger house or to return to the world. So it has been. But I doubt if even the women will be treated softly now. For now the true matter of it has begun . . . Suppression —death . . . The worst may come to us all.'

Simon Mallory, who had been so silent, now stirred and spoke in reply to his brother. His wife and daughters turned to him as flowers to the sun.

'It must be as you say, Roger. The church shall cease building.'

'Thank you, Simon,' said Dom Thomas quietly. 'I know this is best. Pray God, the time will come when the work may safely continue.'

'There, mother,' Simon Mallory said, 'you must needs agree.' He put his hands on her shoulders and pressed them warmly, smiling down at her.

'I am not ruled by you,' she said firmly. 'I accept the truth as your brother has told it, and I ask the rest to accept it, too. And I make my own decision.'

'Well, well, as you please,' Simon said shortly. 'The result is the same.'

His wife, looking at her hands, smoothed her gown on her knee. She smiled her small smile. Perhaps she smiled at her own virtuous and obedient self, who always agreed with every word her husband uttered; perhaps to see him worsted. None would ever know, the Medleys had heard their father say once, whether Mistress Mary's thoughts ran east or west or skitterwaisen between the two . . .

The brightness had long drained from the April day. What had been no more than 'change in the air' had become a suddenly realised threat to a dearly familiar way of life. They were, it had seemed certain, far from any hurly-burly here, busy about their own concerns, engulfed by the quiet forest and the steady inevitability of seasonal affairs. The great upheaval in the state had seemed solemn but remote. And when word of the northern uprising filtered through to places like Mantlemass and Ghylls Hatch and Staglye village, with later news of its crushing, with burnings and hangings and imprisonments, the tumult still seemed to be taking place in some other world. That the King had declared himself head of the Church had shocked and appalled many simple souls, and as many less simple. But the rights and wrongs of it were too difficult to concern the quiet worshippers in ancient churches about this Wealden countryside. For them, rarely diverted from a simple daily routine, God seemed a good deal more familiar than King Henry, or than the Pope who had denied him and defied him by refusing to divorce him from his Queen. Wisely enough, they kept their souls to themselves and said their prayers as usual.

When Master Medley and his three sons had bidden farewell to Dame Cecily and the rest, Dom Thomas came from the house with them. They stepped out on to the flat unwalled courtyard that faced out across the forest, but now the dusk was down and they saw only shadows. They turned in the direction of the promised church, two hundred or so yards from the house, where the foundations and some small works might be seen in spite of the growing dark. The church would not be very big, but it would have a tower with bells, and the south chapel was to be a chantry for the Mallorys, where all who died and were to die would be long remembered, their names and images carved in stone for all to see. But now it must wait.

Dom Thomas and his old friend walked ahead of the three boys, and snatches of their conversation drifted back. Master Medley spoke quietly, and Dom Thomas replied—'Is it to be Judith? Then, Medley, I rejoice. May you be forgiven—it is time!'

'What shall your mother say?'

'She, too—she will be glad.'

'Roger,' the three sons heard their father say, 'the best in the world would be if you marry us. Once, long ago, you said to me—I'll be ordained priest and marry you to your lady. A different lady. You know as I know, Roger Mallory—my good Father Thomas—that when I wed with your sister I had my heaven straightaway then. Maybe we were too happy.'

'Well, may God bless you in your new content, Medley. Come with Judith to the Priory—I'll joyfully see you wed.'

The two men embraced, and Master Medley turned to look for his sons. It was far too dusky to see his face, but all three of them knew that he was smiling.

'Ask your uncle's blessing,' he said to them, as they came closer, 'and let's be gone. The horses are waiting. Judith'll give us a fine dish o'tongues come we're much later.'

His voice had taken on the foresty sound that Richard and Piers loved to hear, that Harry doubted, that Simon Mallory scorned. Medleys and Mallorys both, they spoke two tongues—the one polite and careful and suited to such

as visitors from London and relatives from a richer
world; the other for the forest and forest matters, comfortable, slipshod and full of words that strangers could
not understand.

Piers shoved Richard towards Dom Thomas. Richard
went willingly on his knees, saying 'Father, give me your
blessing.' Piers knelt beside him and eventually, with a
shade of reluctance, Harry joined them. Dom Thomas
said: 'Now may God guide and bless these three sons of
my dearest sister and my oldest friend. Per Christum
dominum nostrum.'

'Amen,' they said, and then walked back to where the
horses were waiting.

Dom Thomas saw them mounted.

'Now I must take my own way home,' he said. 'Before
I go, I ask one thing of you, Medley. A time must surely
come of danger and distress. If I send—I beg you to come
then and help me. For I shall be sore pressed if I call on
you.'

'I give my word for that. And I speak for Piers and
for Harry.'

'And for Richard, sir,' the boy said.

'And for my son Richard, father,' Master Medley
corrected himself; and he made no jest of it, as some
fathers might.

They mounted and rode off into the dark down the
familiar track, and all the way home they none of them
spoke a word.

Judith was at the door when they rode in. She was dark,
thin, small-statured, calm and positive in manner. As
soon as his father had swung him to the ground, Richard
dashed to her.

'Good evening, mother,' he said.

She caught him about the shoulders and muffled his
face against her sleeve, crying 'Hush!' and looking up
over his head at the others.

'No need to hush,' Master Medley said. 'No secret
now, Judith. They know and are happy.'

'Come indoors, then,' she said, stepping back for them, then standing very firmly, waiting for what should be said next.

Master Medley went in first, and taking her hands he kissed her cheek. Then Piers followed, and he, too, kissed her, saying 'Welcome.' Then it was Harry's turn. As he hesitated, Judith made the first move, catching him by the hand. 'We shall do very well,' she said quietly, 'Anne and I. If you think otherly, then she and me are still strangers.' She laughed very fondly as he still resisted her. 'Ah, you gurt gummut, Harry! You don't deserve the maid. She's twice the heart that you have. And I've got twice the sense. So—rest easy.'

Richard pushed the heavy door behind them all. He looked out over the forest through the last crack, and he could still smell the spring. The sky was clear but the wind had risen. It was a cold wind, blowing from the north.

3

A Promise Claimed

'I'll bide here with you, Piers,' Richard said, crouching beside his brother in the straw of Sola's stable.

The mare was on the ground, her head in Piers's lap, and he just sat there stroking and soothing her. She had sickened without warning four days ago. Matthew Ade, the head stableman, said she had a growth in her belly, and he was all for slitting her throat. But Piers could not bring himself to it, either to give the order or to do the thing himself. If any must kill her, then he would—but he still clung stubbornly and stupidly to the hope that she would recover. He had been with her all night, and now it was seven in the morning of Harry's wedding day—for Anne had stayed staunch and her father reasonable, just as Judith had believed.

'I'll stay,' insisted Richard, for his brother had not answered. 'Long as you do. Long as she do, poor beast.'

'You must go to the feast, Dickory. That's for sure. And best you get in now and clean yourself, and get dight up in that fine doublet Judith find you.'

'I'll be grieving all the time—'

'A wedding's for jollity. So you be jolly. Go on—get off with you.'

Richard still lingered. He put his hand on Sola's hard cheek, sadly enough, for she had never let him near her. Her eyes were open, the lashes flat and gummy. Her nostrils blew gently and irregularly.

'Does it pain her, Piers? Does it?'

'She'm past pain, I reckon,' Piers said harshly.

'She must die, then—must she?'

Piers did not answer. His throat swelled and his eyes filled with bitter tears. Sola was too young to die; yet all she had had of life she owed to him and his careful rearing of her, and perhaps that must be his comfort.

'Harry'll look for you,' Richard said, rising to his feet at last and turning away from his brother's grief.

'He'll see it my way.'

'And our father, Piers—?'

'He always understand.'

'Then I'll go,' said Richard.

'Kiss Anne for me, and wish her joy.'

'I will. And tell her why I do it.'

'I'll ride after—soon as I may, but I won't say when.'

The boy left the stable, letting in a shaft of winter sunlight. The year with its strange and mounting troubles, only half understood, had moved on into November. This time last month the mood had lifted wondrously, for the King became father of a son by his third wife, Queen Jane. Beacons had blazed along the hill tops, and were barely quenched before the bells began tolling for the death of the infant prince's mother . . .

The mare shifted slightly, her hoofs scrabbling helplessly along the stone floor and sending up a cloud of chaff.

'Ah, Sola, we rid so far together,' Piers said to her. 'Who'll carry me now? We never did ride hard, but always sure and steady. None'll take me over the platty ground the dainty way you done.' She shifted again, as if settling more comfortably against his knee, and closed her eyes slowly, sighing. 'Rest a bit, my beauty,' he urged her.

Now all was quiet, for the wedding party had ridden away, Harry the bridegroom in the lead, Master Medley and Judith his wife riding next, and Richard close on his white pony, Argent. Then came a train of ten servants in new liveries, two and two, and a pack horse with gifts. Piers thought of it miserably. He, too, had a new doublet to wear and when should he do so now? There were few enough chances, he thought, for any of them to dress up gumptious. Disappointment added to his deep wretchedness over the mare, and the whole world seemed to darken.

He heard someone striding over the yard, and then Matthew Ade came into the stable and over to Sola's stall.

'You should let her go, sir,' Matthew said. 'She look proper gabby in the face now—anyone see that. Let her go, Master Piers. I'll do it for you quick as light. She'm too far gone to feel it.'

Before Piers could answer there was the sound of voices outside. The door was shoved open and a man came in, one of the young grooms catching at his sleeve and trying to pull him back.

'I did try to hinder him, sir,' the lad cried. 'I should'a said you was from home.'

Piers looked up at the stranger, who had the appearance of having ridden hard. He was pale, very short of breath, and something about him struck Piers as familiar in a way he could not quite understand.

'Send the man away, Piers Medley,' the newcomer said. 'I've a message from your uncle at St Pancras Priory.'

Piers recognised him then, and with a great sense of shock. For this was Brother Hilary, the Priory porter, only he was not wearing his habit, but decent riding boots and a cloak over a fustian doublet. The instant that Piers absorbed this, coming out of his preoccupation with Sola so abruptly that it was like plunging his face into cold water, he knew what Brother Hilary's message would be.

'All right, then,' he said to Matthew and the lad, nodding them towards the door. 'Now, brother?'

'You know me?'

'I know your face. The rest's strange enough.'

'We have great need of help, my son. It was your father I was sent for—but any Medley would hear me, so Dom Thomas said.'

'Hear what?'

'The Prior is to give his charge over to the King's Commissioners. The Priory is forfeit. There is no choice—or there is a choice that could mean death for all of us. The Prior will not sacrifice his brethren—and, God help us, we are not all the stuff of martyrs.'

'What am I to do, then?' Piers asked, still sitting there in the straw and frowning up at Brother Hilary. 'What help? And where? And when?'

'It must be now,' said the monk, crouching beside Piers. 'All our treasures and relics are forfeit. The coffins of our founders are buried deep—they may escape desecration. But there's one thing Dom Thomas is set to save. It is the great portrait on brass of Prior Nelond. It is over a hundred years old and there is none more wonderful. You have heard how such wonders are being defaced and mutilated and destroyed all about the country . . .'

'Is there no help in the town?' Piers asked, bewildered by the passionate urgency in Brother Hilary's voice. 'If it were destroyed—well, it was made by man, surelye.'

'Dom Thomas has a particular devotion to the memory of Prior Nelond. It was looking at the great portrait, he says, that he first knew of his vocation. It was for Prior Nelond that he took the name Thomas—to share with him the same patron, St Thomas of Canterbury. I think you know all this.'

'Yes . . . Some of it.'

'There was a promise, Dom Thomas says.'

'Right enough there was a promise—but not to shift baggage, I think.' He looked now at Brother Hilary eye to eye, seeing terror and despair. 'Is it only the baggage?'

The monk, in his uneasily secular clothes, was sweating. He was neither young, nor athletic, neither martyr nor hero. He had a liverish look. Plain to see, he was frightened out of his wits at what might be coming.

'There will be three of us,' he said. 'And the—the baggage, as you call it.' Then he began to gabble. 'We shall none of us return to the Priory. Brother Francis and I will return to the world and manage as best we may. Dom Thomas goes to France—he will not renounce his vows. But he will save the brass portrait first or he will not go at all.' Brother Hilary rubbed his hands over his damp face. 'There you have it.'

'My mare is dying,' Piers said.

Brother Hilary looked as if he had been struck across the face. His chin trembled. He rose unsteadily from his haunches and looked about him vaguely.

'Who can help me . . . Who can I go to . . . If only your father were at home . . .'

'No one is at home. They have all gone to see my brother wed. There'll be feasting and dancing and I know not what frolicking beside. They'll not be home till this time two days, I reckon.'

It was then he thought that his uncle must be hard pressed indeed to have forgotten the marriage, and his conscience seemed to beat in his mind like a second heart. He looked down at poor Sola and found her far more worthy of his care than Brother Hilary. It was his uncle he needed to consider, however, and the promise given, back in the spring, that they had all made through their father—and what would he say, if none honoured it? All the tales of hangings and butchery flooded his memory, and he knew what he had in honesty known from the first. 'Go to the door, brother,' he said, 'and call for Matthew—that was here when you came.'

While the monk went outside, Piers crouched close over Sola, kissing her on the brow. 'Farewell,' he said.

Matthew came hurrying in. If Piers was the greatest

lover of horses at Ghylls Hatch, then Matthew Ade ran
him a good second. His concern for Sola made him scowl
anxiously.

'It has to be done, Matthew,' Piers said. 'Hold her
head.'

Matthew knelt down and took Sola's head in his hands
to steady it, but the head lolled heavily away.

'Leave your knife sheathed, Master Piers,' he said.
'There's no need of it now. She'm gone.'

Piers stood up at once, and did not look at Sola at all.

'What do you need?' he asked Brother Hilary.

'A cart or a waggon . . .'

'To be druv where?'

'To the north-west some miles. Prior Nelond's family
was settled there, so there he must return.'

'Ride back, then. Tell my uncle the promise is
redeemed.'

'Come by night, my son.'

'By night. And be thankful it's the darks and no light
showing.'

'God bless and keep you,' said poor Brother Hilary,
his voice rough and shaking. He took Piers's hand and
clasped it, then went quickly out of the stable. They
heard him ride away.

'Get two or three of the lads, Matthew,' said Piers,
'and tell them to bring spades. I'll see poor Sola under-
ground before I go.'

It was a long drive with a waggon to pull, and except for
the flare and glare of five or six furnaces against the sky
the night was as dark as pitch. Piers had chosen a horse
accustomed to the way, for they came often enough to the
town; spring and autumn there were the sheep fairs, and
sometimes there was timber or hides to sell—one of the
lads helping to bury Sola had groaned a bit at the loss of
good leather. The waggon rattled and lurched over the
frosty ground, iron hard but with fearsome ruts. It was

only when he was well on the way that Piers began to think at all clearly. Until then he had only muttered to himself about his uncle's pious determination to see Prior Nelond's monument safe from desecration. Now he saw that he was to have a hand in snatching three Benedictine monks from whatever future might have been decided, and that this could be treason. He wondered bleakly if he might be running his own head into a noose for the sake of a sheet of brass, however cunningly engraved. Yet the scent of danger made him lift his head. Indeed, he was the best of those who had promised to undertake the task—his father being only just married, and heart-warmingly content, Harry an even newer bridegroom, and Richard far too young. All the same, with the night about him and the cold striking between his shoulder blades, his spirits began to sink again very fast, and he felt bitterly alone. Nothing and no one stirred in the frost-bound silence, until he came to the river. Then he heard the sound of wings and knew that geese were passing overhead, strung out in long skeins against the sky, travelling none knew where. The birds seemed to pass across in another world, and in yet a third, it seemed to him, the guests at his brother's wedding moved to music and lights and warmth, to laughter and food and drink . . . He crossed the river very shortly and soon he saw the Priory buildings black against a sky remotely less black over the wide valley. He slowed the horse to a walk and made his way to the side of the building that fronted on the marshes, a little salty from the nearness of the sea's full tide. He stopped by a low postern door, and immediately it opened and he heard his uncle's voice.

'Piers? You're in good time.'

'My father is from home. Else, he would be here.'

'I forgot. A great deal to think about at this time . . . All's ready here. And a fresh horse.'

'Brownie'll goo a hundred mile if I ask him. We only cover fifteen till now.'

'As you think—but I'd start fresh from now.'

'He's bred to the plough. He'll pull for ever. We know one another,' Piers said obstinately. He thought very little of the Priory beasts and preferred any of his own, who responded to his lightest touch, and pricked their ears to his chirrup. If there should be need for haste— he'd sooner have Brownie tired than a stranger with only a mile or two behind him.

'Leave it, then.' Dom Thomas sounded strained and weary. 'All this is in defiance of Father Prior. A strange cracking of my vow of obedience. Yet I know it must be done. For they will tear the place down in time. There shall not be left a stone upon a stone . . .'

At this moment Brother Hilary loomed out of the shadows. He was carrying a dark lantern and from the spot of light it shed Piers saw that he still wore his secular dress—and not only he, but fat Brother Francis and Dom Thomas, too. Piers had never seen his uncle anything but gowned and cowled. He found him now almost a stranger; even his voice, even his dimly seen face, seemed changed.

'Best get loaded and away, father,' Brother Hilary said.

'Have you contrived some packing?'

'Brother Francis has made a great parcel. Your nephew, father, calls it *the baggage*. With straw and sacking and other padding it makes a goodly weight. It will take all of us to hoist it aboard.'

Piers had more than once been shown the great brass tomb-top, with its over life-size figure, its delicate adorn-ments and inscriptions. It was indeed a beautiful thing, and they would have had anxious moments as it was prized from its stone bed, and all as silently as possible. The straw and the sacking were only a part of its protection. The whole thing had then been clapped between boards and securely roped. It was a vast weight to handle. In the cold and the dark, pinching his fingers between the great package and the side of the waggon, not even able to swear because of his company, Piers thought of his friend Robin Halacre, who had little respect for established things—who would laugh heartily, no doubt, if he could see Piers now.

'We could travel faster wi'out him,' Piers said to his uncle. 'We could be quickly at the coast and find you a boat.'

'You shall take me to the coast, but later. If we leave the brass here it'll be defaced and defiled—broken up. The wreckers of our monasteries dearly love all metals. The lead is torn from the roofs and melted down, and sold for the King's treasury.'

'Must it happen here, then?' Piers asked, uneasy at the mounting vehemence of his uncle's manner—as though this business had turned him from a robust man of great humour, as well as piety, into a hot fanatic.

'Fountains and Jervaulx and the rest torn down—and shall this be spared?'

'That's the last knot tied,' Brother Francis said, tugging at the ropes to make sure all was secure, that the treasure would not fall from its place.

'Best we be going, then,' Piers said. There was nothing for it. He must submit to his uncle's wishes, wherever they might lead him.

The Priory being outside the town walls they took the narrow track along that valley where a small river ran fast in winter. It meant a detour, but it was a track used often by the monks, who had farmlands to administer in all the countryside beyond the town. The frost had sharpened in the last hour or two. The track was firm enough, though it barely took the width of the waggon. Piers was aware as he drove Brownie forward through the dark that a wheel might all too easily slide over the lip of the bank. Here they were free of trees and hedgerows and the wide sky arching over the downs gave them a hint of light. A mile or two along the road they turned aside and began to climb the westward trackway over the downs. Like a flame blown upon, the light increased as they mounted. Now the still sleeping town was well behind them. Soon morning had begun. Passing cottages clustered about the farm on the side of the hill, they saw the glimmer of rushlights, the glow of hearths huffed from blackness into flame, they heard the thump and clatter of pails as the milking set the day upon its course. They climbed slowly, and then, as they touched the summit, in the moment before they started down the far side, they saw the weald below them lifted from the valley floor by the uprush of the winter dawn—a false dawn, that flared and faded, dropping the pastures back into place and veiling them in curls of mist.

It was very cold in the open waggon. Piers dragged at his cloak and shivered. Behind him the three men sat on the floor of the waggon. Brother Hilary and Brother Francis sat huddled together for warmth. No one spoke, but there came from Brother Francis a slight sound every now and again, for he was weeping. Dom Thomas sat apart. He seemed unaffected by the cold. His eyes were open and unblinking, his lips moved. After some time he joined Piers, offering to take the reins.

'Best as we are,' Piers said, unwilling to hand Brownie over.

'As you say.'

'Will you go to France, then?' Piers asked.

'And after that to Rome. To be a witness of what is taking place.'

'Shall I tell my father this?'

'Tell him I wish with all my heart I might have seen him to say goodbye.'

It had been light for two hours and more when, the downland well behind them, they drove through forest lands of a kind familiar to Piers. Accustomed to trees and undergrowth about his home, he felt far easier in this sort of shelter. The tracks were difficult, however, and they were obliged to hold to one firmed by the hard frost, though it led them, Dom Thomas thought, a good way too far west.

'There is a road northward clear of the forest. I rode

it once many years ago. We must needs go back on our
tracks. It cannot be helped.'

Brother Francis now wiped his eyes and stirred himself
to ask what Piers had wanted to ask himself.

'How shall we find where to leave our burden?'

'Someone will tell us where the family of Nelond live
now.'

'Father,' said Brother Francis, his voice husky with
tears and embarrassment, 'I will do anything you bid me.
I will follow you to the grave, if need be. But it is all of a
hundred years since Prior Nelond held office. Since then
there has been the plague. And the plague again, and yet
again. What if there is none of his name left?'

'When I first went as a novice of our Order,' Piers
heard his uncle reply, 'I took the name of Thomas that
I might lean upon it and so learn to conquer doubt. I
shall not doubt now. Now drive on, nephew, and let us
be confident.'

So Piers drove on, but his confidence was a good deal
less than his uncle's. For one thing the day was so fast
misting over that he feared they must soon be swallowed
in the kind of dense fog common to this time of year, fog
in which man and beast might walk in blind circles until
they dropped. He was hungry and cursed himself for
bringing neither food nor money—all he had provided in
his haste and distress over Sola was a bag of feed for
Brownie. His three companions were accustomed to
fasting, but Piers's stomach was beginning to revolt and
grumble.

Presently they came out of the forest into cleared
ground, and shortly they saw ahead of them a church
with a farm and a few cottages. The fog was far thicker
here, but the church with its square tower looked as
blunt and solid and reassuring and comfortable as water
in a desert.

'I'll go seek out the priest,' Piers said, 'and ask the way.'

He pulled Brownie in to the side of the road, rough and
narrow as it was, and climbed down. He was stiff and

cold and glad of a chance to stretch his legs. There was some noise of hammering and sawing, so the place was certainly not deserted. There was no movement about the farm or the cottages, which seemed frozen into stillness and silence by the bitter day. The noise came from the church. Piers crossed the graveyard and peered in at the south door. They were building in there, a whole horde of men and boys, renewing and altering the nave, making a fine new aisle beyond a set of high pointed arches. Piers soon picked out the priest, who was toiling with the rest, and went towards him. One by one the workers paused and turned to look at the stranger, and the sounds of masons and carpenters alike ceased gradually until the church was quiet.

The priest, square, squat, red-cheeked and cheerful, had his gown belted up above his hairy calves, and his hands were white with dust from chiselling. He smiled at Piers without reserve.

'God be with you. A traveller? What's your need, my son?'

'How far to Balcombe village, father?'

'A few miles north-east. Where are you from?'

'Lewes way,' said Piers cautiously.

'You've travelled west a bit. Have you companions?'

'Three.'

'And needing food? I'll show you where my house is. You must come inside. It's a poor day for the road.' He wiped his hands down his thighs, adding something more to the dust already powdering his gown. 'Work on, my brethren,' he commanded. 'The days are too short to waste their light.'

As he walked outside with Piers, the noise began again without any show of reluctance.

'Naught else keeps 'em so warm,' the priest said cheerfully. 'Where's your company?'

'A few paces beyond the gate—with the waggon, father.'

'Mercy—there's a crowd to feed!' cried the priest. 'You said three.'

'Three besides me, sir.'

'Then the place is beset with strangers—what d'you know of the horsemen?'

'There are no horsemen—'

But he was wrong. There were indeed two mounted men with Dom Thomas and the others, and some altercation had broken out. On a third mount, a miserable, head-hung creature with its ribs all showing, and led by the smaller of the two men, a young woman was perched. Dom Thomas was out of the waggon and striding towards this third beast, but the larger and more commanding of the two horsemen—though both were shabby enough— pulled his horse round and barred the way.

'Let be!' Piers heard his uncle say. 'I will speak with her. She called to me for help.'

'There's no help you can give her that I can't,' the first rider shouted. He gave a loud laugh. 'Or less, I'd say—*old man*!'

'Mind your tongue,' Dom Thomas rapped out, and made to step quickly round the horse.

At this the man leant out of his saddle and struck him hard across the chest with his whip.

It happened so quickly that Piers, though he had broken instantly into a run, was not half near enough to prevent the blow. He shouted in his turn. Brother Francis and Brother Hilary moved in and dragged Dom Thomas back, but this seemed to enrage the horseman. He rode at them, bellowing and beating about him, shouting abuse. The second man then came to support him, but he was hampered by the led horse, and was obliged to slip the bridle. The instant he did so, the woman dragged the miserable nag's head round and made off down a narrow path among the trees. His attention diverted from his uncle, Piers saw the horse stumble and the woman swept by low branches from the saddle and thrown to the ground. She was up in a second but fell again as if in pain. He saw her briefly before the log hid her, half crawling, half running among the mist-hung trees, while the horse plunged and snorted, bridle trailing.

'God save us all,' the priest was muttering as he pelted behind Piers. 'Mother of God help and defend us! Brawling at the gate—that's blasphemy for you!'

Dom Thomas broke from the mêlée and ran at once in pursuit of the obviously injured woman. The fog swallowed him as it had swallowed her. The first of the horsemen, still cursing and shouting, and dragging at the knife in his belt, hurled himself out of the saddle and went plunging after them.

4

A Stranger Brought Home

'Catch the horses!' Piers shouted to Brother Francis. 'And don't let that fellow free!'

He ran on himself without waiting to see if fat Brother Francis was less confused than Brother Hilary—in any case he trusted to the parish priest to help them both, for he seemed sturdy enough for ten. Piers went straight into blindness, for the fog hung thick between the trees. Almost at once he slapped into a huddle of saplings and their thin, whippy branches slashed his cheek. Behind him there was a great crashing and panting. Brother Francis was lumbering in support, but there was no time to discover what he had achieved before he followed.

Piers stopped dead and Brother Francis all but knocked him over, he was so closely pursuing.

'Be still—listen!' Piers urged.

It took time for the silence to re-settle, and then immediately it was silence no more, for they heard shouts, and a woman's high scream, and a great trampling somewhere out of sight.

'To the left,' Brother Francis said, his breath seeming to drag itself up out of his great chest only to explode in steam about his head.

'The right,' said Piers.

'Truly, I am a little deaf,' Brother Francis agreed, humble and apologetic.

'You'll kill yourself, come you keep on running so. Come after more slowly. I'll shout if I need you to hurry.'

Without waiting for any protest, Piers went on and the sounds at once grew louder. Then the figures came out of the mist like arrows from a bow. His uncle was in the lead, dragging the girl along, trying to support her as she sagged and staggered and moaned. No more than a few yards behind, the tall figure of their pursuer loomed up giant-like, magically increased in stature by the fog. He shouted as he came—at Dom Thomas to stop and deliver up his prize, at his fellow to come quickly to aid him. This cry was answered, but faintly, and it was clear that the second man at large again had quite lost himself in the fog.

Piers shouted in his turn—'This way! Come this way!' And he snatched up a fallen bough and broke it to cudgel size as he saw his uncle veer in his direction. Then he shouted again, yelled it at the top of his voice—'Have a care! For God's sake—'

The girl had tripped on a thin fallen branch, no more than a handspan round, half buried in dead leaves. Dom Thomas tried to drag her to her feet, then feeling their pursuer closing up, he flung himself down to protect the girl. He was less than a second too late. The man fell in his turn, spreading his arms to save himself. He had a knife in his right hand and it drove straight into Dom Thomas's unprotected back somewhere below the ribs.

For an instant of time everything froze for Piers into a picture drawn in black on milky vellum. Then the colour came back into the picture, the raging red of anger and blood, of hatred that flared and instantly paled into terror.

The picture broke into movement. The wood suddenly

47

filled with trampling and shouting as the workers sum-
moned by the priest from within the church appeared
brandishing the weapons offered by their trades—
hammers, chisels, trowels, mallets. The noise brought the
murderer to his senses and he heaved himself up, retriev-
ing the knife, then turning swiftly into the fog, roaring for
his fellow. One of the workmen must have seen him, for
there came a great hallooing. The hunt gathered itself and
was away. This part of the wood was silent, even before
Piers had reached his uncle and dragged him into his
arms. The girl shrank away as she was released, and Piers
was just aware of her crouching and shaking, her hands
fumbling over her face and her eyes wide and blank with
terror. It was an immense, false silence that descended on
the three together there, beyond which there moved
soundlessly a world full of murderers and hunters after
vengeance—a world of no importance whatsoever.

'Father,' Piers managed. 'Uncle Roger, sir—are you
much hurt?' He knew he was slain but he fought against
it. 'Sir, can you hear me? Speak, if you are able. Speak, I
beg you—I beg you . . .'

At that Dom Thomas slowly opened his eyes, forcing up
the lids as if they were weighted with rocks. He moved his
hand vaguely. The girl seemed to understand this, for she
put her hand in his and began to weep loudly and bitterly.

'By the wounds of Christ,' Dom Thomas wheezed
through the blood bubbling in his lungs, 'I charge you,
Piers Medley—take her—protect her . . .' He ceased,
then, for the blood was in his mouth, but his eyes searched
his nephew's face for an answer, for an assurance.

Muddled and unsure, Piers was bound to give what
was asked for. He said, 'Yes. Yes. I will.' His uncle's
fingers groped at his wrist, insistent, so that he knew he
had not said enough. 'I swear it,' Piers said, and he fumbled
about in his mind for something to make the oath strong
enough to comfort a dying man. 'On—on my mother's
sainted soul,' he managed. 'Her that was your dearest
sister . . .'

48

It seemed to him that his uncle smiled, though it was a strange grimace to give so gentle a name. His eyes closed, his hands relaxed their grip. He died without speaking again.

The fog increased and persisted, that day and the next and into the third. Piers had never travelled so far west before and now he had to find his way home without help or companionship. After all that had to be done for the dead man, the grave dug in the frosty ground, the sad service of committal, it was found that Brother Hilary and Brother Francis had vanished as quietly and completely as the murderer and his companion. Perhaps the brothers should not be blamed, things being what they were, their Priory in dissolution, so much danger in the air. But setting out at last for Ghylls Hatch on a way he did not know and could not see for more than a yard or two, Piers felt as near to despair as any of his age might get. If he could have seen the line of the downs somewhere away on his right hand he would have known, at least, that he was travelling in an easterly direction. He could have managed, then, he thought, as he struggled into the third day—though the tracks where he found himself were heavy with winter, and now if he stuck in a rut or struck against a suddenly looming bank, he had only himself for help. The horse, setting off in good heart after a dry stall and oats at the church farm, was now exhausted by the going. Piers himself had used up all but a remnant of the food that had been pressed upon him for the journey. And over and above all this, feeding a terrible resentment in him, there was the unasked-for burden of the injured woman lying on the floor of the waggon. For a time after the disaster she had lain quite senseless, and he had found himself hoping and wishing that she might have died, and so his responsibility would end. But she stirred and woke and there was nothing for it but to take her with him. She had straw for her bed and her covering was the great

mass of sacking that had been packed round Prior
Nelond's brass memorial. The priest had cried out in
wonder at the sight of it, and taken it to hide in the crypt
of his church—until danger was past, he had said. Piers
did not care what befell Prior Nelond—what was brass
and engraving compared with a man's life? And if there
had to be death, why in the name of God could it not have
been heroic? But for the great brass portrait they need
never have crossed the path of murderers; but for murder
there would have been no vow to care faithfully for a girl
who seemed little better than a slobbering idiot. Plodding
on uncertainly through the fog, Piers's furious grief at the
loss of his uncle made him groan aloud, and blame himself
for the folly and the waste. He had not been quick enough,
he thought. If the fog had not confused him, if the wood
had been less dense with undergrowth, if a branch had
not fallen across that path perhaps two winters ago, if
Brother Hilary had not lagged behind and Brother
Francis had had more breath in his labouring lungs . . .
There were too many ifs to count, and anyway it was a
fruitless exercise. He tried to rouse himself to deal with
more immediate worries.

Early on that third morning he had come upon a
woman milking in an open-sided shed, and she had been
willing to let him have enough for himself and the girl.
He gave her his hunting knife, for he had bartered his
good leather belt for bread the evening before. So now he
was left with nothing for defence but the solid cudgel that
was kept always in the waggon. At noon that day there
was some milk left in a battered and ancient crock the
woman had parted with rather reluctantly, and some nuts
he had turned up by accident when the wheel dug into a
bank and uncovered what must have been a squirrel's
horde. He halted the waggon at a streamside. The fog had
not so much lifted as become paler, so some light must be
filtering into the upper air. He unhitched Brownie and
took him to the water. He had some oats left and gave him
those, fetching the feed from the waggon but not so much

as glancing at the young woman lying there, for he thought in his bitterness he might have spat at her.

'Now, Brownie,' he said, his hand on the horse's neck, 'you pray, too, that we find ourselves soon—else it must be too late and we'll all die together. Goo on, now,' he said, 'get to your prayers while I see to her that's come with us, God help us.'

He went back to the waggon. The girl had roused and had dragged herself to a sitting position in the straw, holding on to her ankle with both hands—she had injured it when she fell from the horse, and now it was greatly swollen. She was paler than any woman he had ever seen in his life. Her face was dirty, besides, smeared and grimed where the tears had poured down and been wiped away. Her dark grey dress was torn, stained with mud halfway to the knee, and spattered with blood. Her head was muffled in a kerchief once white, but now little more than a filthy rag. Most of all, her enormous, dead-looking eyes unnerved him. She seemed scarcely human, and the fact that she would not or could not speak increased his conviction that he was struggling home with some witless thing. Yet with it all he knew most certainly that she must have spoken more to his uncle than that first cry for help. Something she had told him had caused him to bind Piers to care for her, not with a mere promise, but with a sacred oath.

He pulled out the crock of milk and was relieved to find how little had been slopped away by the jolting of the waggon. The jolting had had another effect, however; in spite of the cold, the milk had curdled.

'Here,' he said, thrusting the crock into her hands. 'Drink it.'

She did as she was told, but she was very weak, and the milk added to the general mess by dribbling down her chin.

'That was my own uncle, my mother's brother, died for you,' he said, hating her. 'A good and holy man—master of novices at the Priory of St Pancras—did you know that?

My father's oldest friend—his dearest friend. How'll I tell them what took him? Best speak up for yourself, mistress, or you'll get a thin welcome.'

She stared at him. Nothing in her face told him that she understood, but her fingers tightened and curled on the crock she was holding, so he knew she heard what he said, and the bitter tone in which it was spoken. Dumb she might choose to appear, but she certainly was not deaf as well.

'Why should a man like him die for such as you?' Piers shouted at her in anguish and loss; and she lowered her lids, not quite closing her eyes—that she could not do for she had to let out the tears to wash down her cheeks. 'Oh God forgive me,' he muttered, ashamed. He climbed up into the waggon and took the crock, holding it for her to drink more easily. 'What was it you say to him that make him burden me in this fashion?' he asked more gently. But he expected no answer, and he got none. 'There's a snoule of bread left,' he said, fishing out a remaining crust. 'Take it. We'll need to stop this stiver-about and get home somehow. Else we're beggars for good and all.'

She took a bite of the crust, which was hard and stale, and then held it out to him.

'Isn't it good enough for you, lady?'

For the first time he saw something flash in the depths of her strange blank eyes. So she not only heard but understood. He knew that her gesture had been one of sharing not rejection, so he took the crust and ate it, drank the remains of the milk and shared out the handful of nuts between them. He fetched Brownie and put him back in the shafts. The girl sank down in the straw and huddled under the sacking, moaning to herself when she moved her swollen ankle. He slapped Brownie encouragingly and walked at his head for a while as if to help him on his way. As they went, very wearily now, the trees thinned and the fog thinned, too, lifting and blowing teasingly on a newly risen breeze. An hour or more later, Brownie pricked his ears and increased his pace. They moved right out into the open on highish ground. Away to the south, though still half shrouded, Piers saw the familiar line of the distant downs.

'God be thanked,' he said. 'Brownie smells his home. And so do I.'

The thinning fog turned rosy as the sun set. It lay like a tinted inland sea in every hollow. Then darkness came, and by the time they drove along the track to Ghylls Hatch it seemed like the dead of night. The waggon rumbled over the stones of the yard, the dogs barked wildly, and instantly someone shouted and came running alongside.

'Piers! Piers! Is it you? Are you safe and well?'

'I am safe at least, Richard.'

'Where've you been, brother? None knew and you've been sought all over, hither and yon. Oh dear Lord, Piers,' Richard cried, clasping him thankfully, 'it was most greatly feared some ill had befell you.'

'Some ill did befall, minnow. Is my father indoors?'

'Nay—for he's all set on a great search for you, him and our uncle Simon. Grandmother sits looking pale as stone, and Judith has gone to comfort her.'

'Send a man to Mantlemass, then. Tell 'em I'm home.'

'Harry's here—and our new sister Anne,' Richard said.

'Anne . . .' Piers was so tired that he had to rest his head against Brownie's side. 'I'm not alone. There's a young woman, sick and hurt—in the waggon.'

Before he could say any more in explanation, a door opened and light flooded out. Harry came running and with him Matthew and two or more stable lads, and servants from the house all carrying lanterns, and then what seemed a whole flock of women.

'Piers!' Harry shouted, and seized him and hugged him so rough and hard that Piers's last strength practically went out of him. 'God's truth, we thought you were dead! What's happened? Where have you been these days? It made no sense that you'd vanished.'

'Dom Thomas sent for me . . .' Then he saw Anne hesitating with two or three of the Ghylls Hatch maids behind her, all eyes. 'Sister,' said Piers, 'I've brought a sick woman home. She must be tended.'

Anne came forward. She was a plump girl with fair hair and when she smiled, however shyly, a dimple came into her left cheek. She was wearing a fine new gown, as might any young bride, so she looked rather grand for Ghylls Hatch, where everyone worked with his hands in one way or another.

'My dear brother Piers,' she said, 'you were missed at the wedding. Oh—and since! Praise be you are returned . . . A woman, you said. What manner of woman?'

'A sick woman,' Piers repeated.

'In the waggon, Anne,' Harry cried. He called to the maids, 'Deb—Bessie—see to it.' He still had his arm about Piers, and indeed was half supporting him. 'Who is she, brother? What have you been at?' He was chuckling now and in his bridegroom's mood he gave Piers a nudge in the ribs. 'Where did you find her?'

'She was given me,' Piers said bitterly. 'A trust, Harry. A sacred trust.'

Two of the men had climbed into the waggon and now the girl was lifted out like a parcel.

'Poor thing! Poor thing!' cried Anne eagerly, anxious no doubt to make up for that first hesitation. 'Inside at once—oh, mind how you carry her—she's hurt!' She bustled alongside. 'Bring her in—bring her to the warm.'

They all surged forward, Anne all fuss and flurry, the maids twittering together like starlings, and the girl herself so silent and helpless as to seem out of her senses. Now they were in the hall, where there was light enough to see her as she was laid on the settle. The sacking fell away and they all saw her muddy, blood-spattered dress, her smeared face, her dirty headkerchief and her terrible despairing eyes.

'Lord save us,' Harry muttered. 'What a'God's name have you brought home?'

'She do look scarcey-witted,' Richard said under his breath.

For a second Anne was checked by what she saw, her outstretched hands were drawn back and looked a little as if they might vanish behind her skirts. Piers watched her. He had doubted her once and he feared he would judge her finally and summarily by what she did next. That second fractional hesitation seemed to last for ever. Harry had put out his hand to catch Anne by the sleeve, to absolve her if needed of all responsibility in this extra-ordinary matter. In that instant she moved, and she moved forward. She sank down beside the settle and caught the girl's dirty hands, then touched her poor face in sincere wonder and pity at the wretchedness she saw.

Then she acted as was reasonable for the wife of the eldest son in the absence of the mistress of the house.

'Fetch me a wool coverlet, Bessie. Deb, see a bed prepared—and warm it well. Get to the kitchen, Joan—we need broth or hot milk and some bread to sop in it. Make haste, the lot of you. And a hot brick for her feet, and some pillows here, if you please.'

Piers said quietly, 'You wed the right maid, Harry.'

'So I did indeed,' Harry answered, smiling.

Anne looked earnestly into the girl's filthy face. 'Where are you from? What has befell you? You look a true mawkin, but you have the hands of a gentlewoman for all their grime. What am I to call you?'

'She will not speak,' Piers said.

'She is dumb?'

'No—I know for sure she must've spoke twice. But never since.'

'But how does she come here, brother?' Anne cried.

'For pity, Anne,' Piers said, very faint now, 'let me eat and drink first. I'll tell all when my father come from Mantlemass . . .' He caught at Harry to steady himself. 'Hunger always make me go swimey . . .'

Dreading what he had to tell, Piers rose to greet his father when he strode in half an hour later, with Judith at his elbow. Master Medley clasped and embraced his son, but then, having been in great stress and anxiety for the past many hours, he drew back and thundered, and brought his fist down hard on the table top. But then again his manner changed abruptly and he cried out in great alarm, 'Your clothes are bloodied!'

'Are you hurt?' Judith asked, moving swiftly as if to help him.

'No, madam—leastways, not in my body. The blood is not mine.'

'Whose, then?' his father demanded. 'You've been brawling, have you? You jinked yourself out of your brother's marriage feast—and then went roaring about the countryside like a cut-throat! You have wild friends and they'll do you a harm. Robin Halacre will end on the gallows unless he take good heed.'

'Father—Robin is away in Oxford. And did Matthew never tell you I was sent for?'

'He said a strange man came calling . . .'

'I was sent for, sir. The promise made to my uncle . . . He sent for help. You were not here, nor Harry. Who was to keep the pledge if I stayed timmersome at home? He is dead, father—he is dead. This is his blood on my sleeve. He died as I held him.'

Piers could not bear to see his father's stricken face, nor how he turned even from Judith in her need to comfort him. The tale came out thin and halting, so foolish in its fatal unfolding—the great brass from Prior Nelond's tomb that had been saved at such a cost, the fog that sent them off their way, the casual arrival of the horsemen, the girl's cry for help, the insults and the fury and the pursuit into the misted trees, the dreadful end . . .

'Judith,' Piers said, when his father did not speak, 'pray you go to Anne and see what best to do. I have brought a stranger home. I swore a great oath I would see this woman safe, father. It was what he wanted. There was no other way. I'd have left her if I could. He laid the charge on me—I swore to honour it—I swore on my mother's soul. He was dying and there was no way else. He went so fast . . .'

Master Medley groaned and covered his face. He sat down by the hearth and grief was so heavy on his shoulders they seemed as bent as the shoulders of an old, old man.

'Ah, Roger,' he said very quietly, 'Roger Mallory, my good brother, my dearest friend . . . What are these times that can slay such a man?' Again Judith moved to him, but he waved her away. 'Go to Anne,' he said. 'We are bound to do as he wished us to do. We must nourish the stranger.' Judith went away, and for a time there was silence. 'God rest his dear soul,' Medley said at last. 'I loved him since we were schoolfellows together. He gave me this place we call home, Piers. I never have spoken of this because it was not his wish. When he gave up all he possessed and went into the Church, he made me his heir. Ghylls Hatch would have been his inheritance from his godfather . . . So I brought your mother here when we were wed. But for that gift of his I could have offered nothing but myself, good or bad. Under the roof he gave us my children were born and my wife took her death. Piers, Piers—I shall miss him sore!' He broke into the rough familiar speech of the forester he would always be. 'I dunnamany times I thank him for it, but I'm dubersome he ever give it a thought, once done. He were the bettermost man I ever knew draw breath.'

Piers saw that his father was weeping and he knew there was no way to comfort him. He tried to imagine those two boys long ago, sitting at lessons, racing through the forest, sharing pleasures and griefs and quarrels. He thought of them fishing the pool below the forest bank midway between Ghylls Hatch and Mantlemass, where nowadays he and Harry and Richard fished in their turn. He had heard his grandmother tell Richard once that the pool had been a trysting place for her and their grandfather. All that time had been a growing time—the Mantlemass manor getting bigger and busier, the Ghylls Hatch stock and space increasing, the people and the family multiplying—there would be no room to draw breath in that place, Dame Cecily had complained at one time, for she had seen as many as fifty souls in one day going about their business past her boundaries. Only now something had happened in the outer world that was far beyond their comprehension or their care, that had already brought about one personal disaster in however strangely remote a fashion. It must bring other changes, for sure, though none could have said quite how, and none could know how much . . .

'You saw him buried?' Master Medley said at last.

'In that churchyard, sir—'

'One day, please God, we'll have our own church at Mantlemass. And then we'll bring him home.'

Judith returned then, looking strained and concerned.

'For sure that's a strange burden you carried home, Piers. I pray you'll not regret it, for I greatly fear she must have suffered some bad fever and recently—Her hair's cropped short as a nun. If she would only speak to say where she come from! Oh I do pray most hard and earnest she may not be from some bad plague spot—and bringing it here among us . . .'

5

The Twelve Days
of Christmas

For the next several weeks Judith was desperately anxious about her household. At first she questioned the silent stranger continually—Where have you come from? What is your name? Have you had a fever lately—and were you not truly exceeding sick? Have you come from places where the plague has struck? The girl always lowered her eyes, clasped her hands tightly together and was silent, not even nodding her head, nor shaking it. And so it was with other questions, about her family, if she had one—about the men she had been with on the road that day. She had called for help, they reminded her. She had been carried off, then? But from where? And when? They could as well have saved their breath.

'Ask her once more,' Judith said often to Piers. 'She always look for you to come in—you saved her and so she think much of you. Ask her, then.'

'She will not speak. That's all there is to the matter.'

'She understand what I say,' Judith insisted.

'Maybe. But she will not speak.'

Since she could not learn what she needed to know, Judith was forever putting a hand on the brow of one or the other, turning their palms to see if they sweated, pouring them draughts, both sweet and bitter, from old recipes taught to her years ago by Master Medley's mother, Anis Bostle—Judith had kept house for old Tom Bostle, Anis's father. She never let them rest, they all complained. Thank God, by Christmas time they were all in good health and spirits, and Judith felt able to conclude these ministrations. So they could celebrate the feast of the Nativity with easy minds. Their hearts were a shade less easy. The cloud cast by the brutal death of Dom Thomas still hung over them. An uneasiness remained, an uncertainty and puzzlement as to what might happen next. In the second week in November, the Benedictine Priory of St Pancras had been formally handed over to the King's commissioners; the prior and the brothers were dispersed, as casually as soldiers disbanded after war. They would never reassemble, nor would their voices be heard again in the great church, singing the daily office round the clock from dawn to sunset and to dawn again. The great buildings stood empty, locked and barred against the curious or the light-fingered. Nothing stirred there, but the pigeons in the lofts, which, accustomed to be fed for winter meat, began to raid the grain stores round about. Two days before Christmas word went round that the priest at Staglye had vanished. He left no word, his house was empty with the door swung open. No one had news of him, and without him there was none to say a Christmas mass. His parishioners were bound to go elsewhere, tramping or riding into neighbouring parishes . . .

The Medleys kept the feast at Mantlemass, where Dame Cecily still took the head of the table—a place she had not yet so much as hinted at giving up to her son Simon, though he was lord of the manor now. It had been Judith's idea to take the silent stranger along with them to Mantlemass. She had recovered in health, though she

still limped a little, and she was icy pale. Judith was convinced that if any might persuade the girl to speak, then
Dame Cecily was the one. And she tried; tirelessly and
gently, all that day she tried but failed. In the evening, in
the hall hung with evergreen boughs, they had music and
dancing as they had done since Dame Elizabeth's day.
But the girl sat apart, and though even Richard took her
hand and tried to lead her out, she would not budge.
Perhaps her ankle still pained her—but no one really
accepted this as the reason for her refusals, her persistent
head-shaking. It was something, indeed, that when she
shook her head at Richard she smiled a little.

Richard's three Mallory cousins clustered round him,
so he was bound to choose one of them instead.

'Is she bewitched?' asked Margaret.

'Has she lost her wits?' demanded Elizabeth.

'Poor thing—I hope she may find her tongue,' said
Susannah.

So Richard chose Susannah because she sounded kind.

Piers watched all this in anger and self-loathing, for he
felt himself responsible for laying this burden on the
household. The business had made him short-tempered,
often sullen—a completely alien mood. He knew he could
have done no other, yet blamed himself that he had found
no way out of the dilemma. He wanted the stranger gone,
for she was a perpetual menace to his peace of mind. He
had even found himself wishing most fervently that Dom
Thomas had died, if he had to die, without time to place
this charge upon his nephew. No one had suggested that
he could have done anything but accept the burden—
how could they? There was room enough for more than
one such stranger to be absorbed into the Ghylls Hatch
household. But everyone there had his place and his task,
there was a constant hum of activity indoors and out.
They lived, Harry sometimes complained, more like
peasantry than gentlefolk, rising at first light and going
early to bed. It was essential that the newcomer be given
some identity—but what could it be? Neither guest nor

servant, she sat in remote corners with her hands folded and often her eyes closed. No single word of impatience had come from any one of them save Piers. They accepted that without in any way knowing why, they cared for her for the dead man's sake. He had known, when he asked Piers to cherish her, why he had done so—but he could never tell them why . . .

Susannah Mallory was eight years old, and her hands were warm and sticky from eating sweetmeats. She danced with a gay solemnity, careful and neat but smiling with pleasure that she, the youngest, had been chosen by Richard—and wickedly delighted with the glowering looks of her neglected sisters still sitting by the wall.

'Only my sister Anne—my new sister—of all this company dances better than you,' Richard told her, speaking politely and carefully as he seldom bothered to at home. 'She is a very fair young dame, I think. You, Cousin Susannah, are a very fair young damsel.'

This made Susannah giggle so much she missed a step and almost fell, and Richard only just saved them both from crashing to the floor.

Just then the music broke into a jig, a country dance that set them all shouting and changing partners. Only Mary, Simon Mallory's prim wife, stayed strictly with her husband, the rest shifted about at the end of every round. Piers, with a little too much wine inside him for sense, approached the stranger. She was the only one of them all left sitting—the most ancient servant of the house, the youngest guest all skipped and wove in hand-linked chains about the hall. Without waiting for her refusal, Piers seized the girl's hands and tugged her to her feet. Before she knew it he had whirled her into the centre of the chain, so that she was turned and twisted and spun. Everyone was laughing, and when they saw her they cried out in kind encouragement, and clapped their hands to her. Piers kept at her elbow, guiding and supporting her. She was making no steps at all, but moving helplessly against the rhythm, hampered indeed by her slight limp, but not by that alone. She was a dead weight as he pulled her round, but suddenly she seemed to catch the beat. At last her feet moved as they should, even the little limping hesitation was gone, she grew light against his arm as the music lifted and carried her and she took her heels from the ground and pointed her toe. It was only when the music ended and the whole company was boisterously laughing and clapping and shouting for more, that she struggled away and pushed through the throng and vanished out of the hall.

'There now!' cried Anne. 'You've offended the poor creature!' But she was too excited and too happy to stop laughing.

'The devil take her snivelling solemnity!' shouted Piers, stumbling and stammering over the words. Everyone spun round to look at him, but the music began again, and they forgot him as they rushed to take partners—though Judith did pause at his side.

'You're drunk, surelye! Keep out of your father's sight. You think you're a man but he'll only see a sottish lad. He'll swinge you soon as look at you, for all your grand airs. Get outside into the cool. You're not old enough yetner to take so much wine.'

'To hell,' said Piers, rude and angry, shoving through the crowd. This one and that caught at his sleeve, but he thrust them all off and left the hall. He went through to the kitchen and flung the door open and stepped into the yard. The girl was there ahead of him, sitting on the rim of the well, her face bent into her hands, and she was weeping most bitterly.

The confused anger in Piers made him shout at her— to hold up her head, to summon her good sense, to behave like any other of God's creatures.

'Whatever and whoever you may be, a swineherd's child, or a nobleman's daughter, or the silliest of all here—look up and live your life among us—if it must be among us. Else go and leave us and let us all be free of you and the charge Dom Thomas unfairly set upon me to

keep you. Be one of us—or go! Go!' The words poured
out of him—he sounded like anyone but himself—but he
could not stop them being spoken, being shouted rudely
and bitterly and loudly.

She took her hands from her face and looked at Piers.
Though her cheeks were blotched and her eyes swollen,
he was bound to see how she was recovered in health and
in appearance; he had barely given her a straight look
since he brought her home muddied and dirty, for by not
looking he seemed to deny her existence and his own
unformed fears. Now he was bound to recognise that
there was a terrible anguish about her—not only in her
face, but somehow in the way she held her shoulders.
Anne had lent her a dark red gown and between them all
the women had stitched new linen caps for her. Now her
cap had fallen back a little, showing her hair, which
Judith had said was good as shaved when she came. It
had grown in the past weeks and appeared now softly
brown and silky and twisting into curls on her brow.
Piers stood before her, with his anger and his resentment,
his contempt of himself, his curious fear of her, all boiling
and fermenting inside him. A violent pity took him,
sweeping away all the rest—pity for her or pity for
himself, he was uncertain which—but it rose in him in a
terrible wave of sickness. He staggered across the yard
and through the gate in the wall. As soon as he was in the
darkness outside, a breeze on his forehead, and the rattling
of dry winter grasses in his ears, he was obliged to stand
and vomit. Wine and passion went out of him together
and left him shivering with cold and humiliation.

Piers did not return to the hall and the merriment
there. He went out to the stables, where only one very
old man stayed by his lantern till the guests came for
their horses.

'Say I am sick and gone home,' Piers ordered, 'that I
took swimey and saw best to leave.'

'The young's as weak-headed as sheep,' the old man
muttered.

'Give my message, you poor wind-shaken crittur,' Piers
said, trembling with cold and hearing his teeth chattering.

'You'll not get a-saddle if you try,' the old man said.
'Look, master—climb up into the loft and let you sleep
an hour. The straw's sweet and you'll wake all fine and
ready to get back to the yoistering, if it still be doing.'

The understanding, easy kindness of the old servant
filled Piers with an even deeper despair of himself. He
crawled up the ladder and fell into the straw. It was not
old enough to be musty, but sweet and scented with all
the remembrance of last harvest time and dry as bleached
bones. His head went down, spinning and swimming, and
he did not know which way up he settled. There was no
time for him to ponder the question, for either he fainted
and then slid into a deep sleep, or slept without any
preamble. When he woke it was long after midnight, the
guests were going home, the horses stamping—bad-
tempered, he thought, at being roused. And why should
not all have stayed till morning? It must be Mistress
Mary who sent them all packing from the hall, sweeping
them out as she would see the green boughs swept on
Twelfth Night. 'She keep the place sadly neat,' his
grandmother had once complained.

He tumbled down the ladder, his head clear now as the
moonlight that greeted him when he stepped outside.
Every leaf and twig was white with frost on which the
moonlight superbly glittered. Still wildly merry from the
splendours of the evening, Harry and Anne and Richard
were already mounted and chasing one another in and
out of the great trees that stood sparsely a little above the
house.

'Piers—are you whole again?' It was his father calling
to him. He was laughing after all, whatever Judith may
have said. 'Home, now! It's time for bed—high time.'

As they moved off, Piers nudged his horse up to ride
alongside his father.

'I am very sorry, sir,' he said. 'You have a sadly sottish
son.'

'I'll have him once, Piers, but not again. So—mind it.
Mind it, boy . . . Lord, Lord—I'm getting old. I feel
done-over enough to fall sleeping in the dick!'

He looked sideways at Piers and the moon was bright
enough for his son to see his face. He looked a young man,
whatever he said—younger, indeed, since his marriage.
He was smiling slightly, and Piers, still rather sheepish,
smiled back. A curious feeling moved in him, one that
he had known often before without quite giving it shape.
With his mind so washed and clear, as it was now, he was
able to put some form to the feeling. It was that he loved
his father as easily as if they were brothers of an age
together—comfortable and familiar and trusting each
other as comrades will. No son, and no father, he thought,
could ask better than that.

Richard woke next morning and sighed to think that
Christmas Day was past. There was still St Stephen, and
the beginning of the New Year, and the feast of the
Epiphany on the twelfth day, but nothing was ever quite
as good as Christmas Day itself. He opened his eyes to the
feeling that ordinary working days had returned. In the
New Year he was to have gone to the school in Southover,
by Lewes, where he would have lodged with the family of
Gilbert Hayler, who had once been saddler at Ghylls
Hatch but now worked for his father-in-law in the town.
The school that had been founded twenty-five years or
so ago by a pious widow, had a master approved, under
the terms of the endowment, by the Prior of St Pancras.
Now that the priory community had been dissolved it
might be that the school would close—though how this
might legally be done was much argued at Ghylls Hatch
and Mantlemass. Master Medley, who had learnt a little
of such matters when he was working years ago under old
Nicholas Forge, the secretary at Mantlemass, had said
the school must surely continue as long as there was
money left to pay for it. Harry, however, the only one of

66

the Medley sons to have lived for a time away from home
—and that in London—was sure that if the bequest
could be broken in one respect, as in the appointment of
an approved master, then it could be broken in other
ways as well. About all this Richard did not know whether
to be glad or sorry, or which for which. He might like to
venture a bit into the world, work alongside lads of his
own age, learn something of the swaggering town—but
how would he bear being parted from Piers and the rest
of them, and no longer able to step out of the door and
find the forest waiting? He would ride home on holidays
and Sundays, they had told him—but that was bound to
depend on the weather and the state of the roads.

It was early when Richard woke. It was cockcrow, and
the call was being taken up all around and on into the
distance. Richard felt as if he had only just tumbled into
bed and he groaned as he turned under the covers. He
shared room and bed with Piers, who was already up,
yawning and fumbling at lacing his everyday leather jerkin.
It was just possible to see him against the square of the
windowpane, for the last of the moon was still in the sky.

'Dickory?' said Piers quietly, pausing at the movement
in the bed.

'Aye,' said Richard, and groaned again.

'Put your head in the pillowbere,' Piers advised. 'I'll
tell 'em you've slept over. I'll say your prayers for you.'

'Hmmmmm,' said Richard, burying his face and
sleeping again as he heard Piers laugh.

Later, he woke and it was light. Down below in the
hall there was a tumult. Harry was angry and letting them
all know about it, his deep voice rumbling and then rising
to a roar. Piers answered, sharper and lighter. Judith
spoke. There was Anne's voice, and she seemed to be
crying. Richard dragged himself out of the warm bed,
huddled into his clothes and went fast downstairs. They
were still arguing when he got there, Harry sitting and
pulling on his boots, Anne crying into her hands—and
Judith holding Piers by his arms, firm above the elbow,

shaking him like a baby, for all she was half his size.
'You stay at home with the women! It's your yammer-
ing that's to blame. It was you frit her, with your blustery
talk. Now we've to waste work and time to find her and
fetch her back.'

Piers shouted so that Richard almost jumped out his
skin. 'Let her go! Let her go!'

'May God forgive you, Piers Medley!' shrilled Anne.
'The poor creature—the poor silly thing! What if she fall
into some black hole, out on the fearful forest?'

Richard looked about for his father to quell the tumult,
then remembered why he was not there. He had agreed
to go hawking with Simon Mallory that morning. They
had planned to take a heron or two, or swan, for the
Twelfth Night supper, and would have been out again
almost as soon as they had fallen into bed, heading before
first light for the marshy lands to the north west. So
without the master everyone shouted as he liked, and the
fuss continued while Harry struggled with his boots, and
shouted for his cloak and gloves. Piers did nothing but
fold his arms and lean against the wall, looking pale and
sullen and curiously frightened—at least so Richard
thought. Outside, Matthew was calling to the stable lads
and there was a stamping of horses in the chilly morning.

'Has something happened?' Richard asked—and sprang
back with his shoulders high because he thought for a
moment that Harry was going to cuff him.

Judith caught him and held him against her.

'One man's as bad as his neighbour,' she said. 'Don't
you fear the grummuts, my dawlin.'

'The quiet girl's gone, Richard,' Anne cried. 'She's
run from us and she never had any but love and pity.
She's gone away—'

'And must be found for the love of God and of Dom
Thomas,' Harry burst out. 'A dying man's trust—and
driven out by cruel discourtesy!'

Matthew was at the door to say that the horses were
ready, and he had mustered five of the men besides

68

himself to ride out searching. Harry looked very fine, Richard thought; his big boots and his anger made him seem a hero. As he stamped out of the hall Anne went twittering after him, catching at his arm, telling him to take care, to ride cautiously, to watch every step, to return safely . . .

'She think the forest's goblin-land,' Richard said. He and Piers were left in the hall, for Judith had followed Anne and then they had gone off together. The trampling, jingling horses were out of earshot in no time at all; except for the voices of the women, talking hummingly together behind some distant door, the whole place was suddenly deeply silent. 'You never did mean *Let her go*—did you, Piers?'

'One way, I did. Aye.'

'But not to mean it,' Richard said positively.

Piers straightened himself and kicked a stool near the fire. He sat down as wearily as if he had come riding fifty miles through the deep winter. Richard shifted cautiously towards the hearth, and sat down in the rushes.

'You tell me, Piers,' the boy said.

Piers answered in a mumbling way, more as if he were talking to himself. 'I fear her. What she may be—or what she may do. I never spoke with any like her—and cannot speak with her, neither, come to that. What if she be other than she seem? What then, Dickory?'

'How—other?' Richard asked. 'Bewitched?'

'That I don't know,' Piers said, sounding and looking entirely baffled. 'That's the whole truth of it, brother. I never do know, prensly or nexdy or any other. There, I tell you—that's the only truth I'll swear to.'

'Did you speak *that* to her, Piers?' Richard asked, in awe—for of all things they had been taught courtesy as the virtue most likely to let them into heaven. 'Did you say so to *her*? Right to her face?'

'I said worse,' Piers answered stonily. 'I said Look up, I said, and live decent with us. Else go. Else go, and so we'll be free again.'

'Dear Mother of God!' said Richard, aghast. 'You never should've spoke so rough.'

'Well, so now she's gone, Dickory. And come they find her dead in the cold I'm as good as a murderer.'

'We'll find her,' Richard said, scrambling at once to his feet. 'Come on, Piers. But let's go on our own feet, so we can see close to the ground. She'll not be far. It's not worth horses. The rest'll ride far, but we'll be the ones to find her. But we don't need to waste more time, brother.'

'I cannot,' said Piers, his hands hanging down between his knees as if they were weighted with chains.

'I'll go alone, then. A pity there was no snow last night for tracks. I daresay I'll not be long finding her, though, once I'm into my boots.'

He sounded like a smaller Harry and Piers grinned, then—faintly enough, but he grinned. They went out of the house together some minutes later.

It was a deep and colourless day, the cold striking upward from a ground dank with the heavy wet of frosty nights broken by warmer days. A great shutter of cloud had come up in the last hour or so, and the bright white moon that had seen them home at midnight might have shone from some legendary sky.

'You'll get your snow tonight, latest,' Piers said.

Richard did not answer. He stood only a few yards from the house, questing about like a pointer. Harry and the rest had gone down the narrow way immediately south of the stables, driving an arrow head straight into the body of the forest. But she could have gone any way, for none knew her purpose. It took Richard to see the simplest possibility—that she had gone to seek shelter at Mantlemass where last night Dame Cecily had taken time to wheedle and coax and care for her. For somehow there was too much sense in her silent face for her to go plunging off to what might most likely be her own

destruction. She was devout at her prayers with the rest
of them. She would not for very dread destroy herself.
She would seek help, rather. And the only other place
she had been to in these parts was Mantlemass. It was
as if Richard took command, for Piers followed him
without question as he turned for Mantlemass, though he
lagged a bit. Richard looked sideways at him as they
trudged through the muddy places—the horses went this
way so often the place was rutted more than ankle deep.
They took to the sides and tramped over the broken
bracken, wet and the colour of chestnuts.

Richard stopped suddenly, and without looking at his
brother said flatly, 'What did you mean—about fearing
her? What did you mean in Christian truth?'

Piers paused, too, and they stood there in the quiet
chill morning, with their breath clouding about them.

'More dread than fear, I think. Suddenly the ground
seem all heaving about us, minnow. Dom Thomas dead
and the Priory closed down, and the church at Mantlemass not to build any more . . . And no priest to
minister at Staglye village . . . Someway *she* seem to
come out of it all . . .'

'She come by chance, Piers.'

'Aye, maybe.' He sighed and moved his shoulders,
easing an unseen burden carried there. 'If aught in this
world come by chance.'

'Well, then, God send her where she'd be cared for,'
Richard said positively. 'So there's nothing for us but to
keep her safe.'

'So be it, Sir Richard. Your reverence has shown me
where my duty lie.'

'Don't go mocking, Piers! I never meant to sound
pious.'

'Nor did you—but sensible. You give good advice.'
He struck Richard a soft thump between the shoulder
blades, and then pushed his cap over his eyes. 'Goo on—
goo on, you brat! Get busy forgiving me!'

Richard turned such a loving face that Piers almost

groaned. He strode on at once and Richard had to run to keep up with him. The cloud bank had now moved on and over the whole dome of the sky. Not snow, but a cold rain began. The brothers came up the last bank that rose to a hillock and showed them Mantlemass a quarter of a mile ahead. After that the going was so gentle it was almost flat, for the track shared the wide forest shelf with the manor itself.

By now Piers had convinced himself that they would find the girl at Mantlemass. He strode in with Richard at his heels and crossed the hall calling for his grandmother.

'We've seen nor hide nor hair of her,' Dame Cecily said, after she had rebuked him for the unmannerly noise he was making. 'Why should she run away?'

'Last night I spoke harshly to her. God forgive me, I had drunk too much wine and I was full of fears and furies.'

'However the world goes, it's best to remember manners,' his grandmother said sharply.

'The times confuse and trouble me, madam.'

'They trouble us all. Not least this girl, maybe. You know nothing of what troubles she may have suffered already—something severe, surelye, that she stays so dumb. And if you cannot see as much in her face, you are a greater fool than I guessed. She will speak in time. Have no doubt of that—I have none . . . What does your father say to all this?'

'He left before it was discovered—to go hawking with my uncle.'

'You are bound to find her, Piers. I would take her to live here, most gladly for my dead son's sake. But your father was his dearest friend—he will not want the charge taken from him, I think . . . Now go.'

'Richard'll go with me. And Harry is already out searching.'

'It is a sore day to be about the forest. If she is not found by noon, send word to me. I can spare ten men if need be. But go now—now. I have very little pleasure of your company as things are.'

Once more Richard found himself running to keep up with Piers and he knew by the set of his shoulders he was both angry and bitterly distressed by their grandmother's scolding. Richard felt now that he himself had been too clever by half, that he had failed Piers badly by suggesting that the girl would be at Mantlemass, and more still by coming afoot. They needed horses now. It would be best to beg them here at Mantlemass rather than waste time by going home.

Piers went off at such a rate that he was well on the south-east way from the manor before Richard came close enough to catch his attention. It was here, before the way ran down a gentle slope to join a hollow track from Staglye that they had dug out the shape of the church. It was some four foot high at its eastern end and they had laid a great slab to mark where the altar would stand. The workmen had thrown up a small cove or lean-to within the footings, and there were some tools stored there, mallets and props and suchlike. Somehow the sight of them stacked and idle made the abandonment of the church seem even more distressing. When would men come again and take up the tools and bring more, to dig and build and set up what had been so long planned, and with so much love and devotion . . .

Richard grabbed Piers by the wrist. He jerked his head towards the shelter. 'She's there!' He looked up eagerly into his brother's face and loosed his hold as if he had been burnt. In the second before Piers ran forward, Richard saw as clearly as if it were set out in bright pictures, why his brother had wished the girl gone. He opened his mouth—whether to speak or to cry out in wordless protest he could not know—and perhaps never would, for at that second he heard his name shouted. Harry and the rest came streaming up the track.

'Dickory! There's no sign. I've come to beg men from Mantlemass.'

Richard called back. 'No need. She's found.'

Harry was out of the saddle in an instant, crying 'Where? Where?'

'Yonder. Where Piers is gone . . .'

'Here?' Harry looked around him as if he saw the church already walled and roofed and adorned. 'Poor soul—as if she sought sanctuary!' Then he called out 'Piers! Is all well?'

'Well enough,' Piers answered. He had pulled off his cloak and wrapped it round her and was lifting her. She had been kneeling there, but she had sat back on her heels in weariness or despair, and now she was so cramped and cold she could not walk.

'God be thanked she is alive,' said Harry. He took her hands and rubbed them gently. He looked quickly sideways at Piers. 'I am sorry for my words to you this morning, brother. We're none of us saints.'

'Get her home,' Piers said.

'Mantlemass is nearer.'

'Get her home,' Piers repeated, his voice hard and urgent. '*Get her home.*'

Richard hung in the background. Looking from brother to brother; worried, uncertain. Jealous.

6

The Stones of the Priory

So for the second time they brought the silent stranger to Ghylls Hatch, and this time without hesitation the women of the household cosseted and fussed her, almost crooning over her in their relief at seeing her alive; quite unexasperated by her silence, filled with penitence that she had fled from one of them who should most carefully assure her welfare. How strangely she seemed to have become a part of the household, to have captured their affections, even, as the weakest often will.

'One more time over the threshold,' said Harry to young Richard, 'and she'm set here for always.'

'Should you be glad, brother?'

'Aye why not? But I doubt it should please Piers. His face is against her now, I'd say. He was the one bound to swear her safety. He wishes it had been some other, I think.' Harry frowned and shook his head, puzzling over something too complicated for his straight way of thought. 'If it had to be at all,' he added, sighing slightly at what he did not understand.

Richard mumbled something, turning away as he spoke, so that Harry growled at him to speak up. 'He've no sort of hate for her,' Richard said more loudly; but he had changed the words. He gave Harry a slanting look, but Harry's face was much as usual—slightly guarded, handsome, perhaps a little doubting in the eyes, though this had eased since his marriage so that often they seemed to shine with a surprised content.

'Tell me your thought about her, Dickory,' he said.

But Richard could not say. He could not betray one brother to the other. It was difficult not to answer frankly, for Harry was flattering him by asking what he thought, and Richard swelled with the feeling that he had somehow moved up, that he was nearer in stature to Harry than he had been only a few hours before. With Piers, the difference in their ages seemed not to exist, but to speak in this way with Harry was to be promoted.

'What should they be?' he said; and let the matter lie, sorry that he felt he could not pursue it.

Just then Anne skipped in looking busy and pleased. 'She will be well by morning!' Piers was coming through the door and paused to listen. 'She will be well by morning,' Anne repeated. 'No thanks to some.'

'Oh be silent, Anne,' cried Harry. 'It's not for you to blame or bludgeon. Leave my brother to his own devices.'

Anne looked as if he had slapped her. She gathered up her skirts to run from the room, and her face gathered, too, into lines of childish, tearful rage.

'Nay—no bawling, neither!' Harry shouted. 'I'll not have you all blotched up with tears. Devil take it, girl, what make you so quarrelsome?'

He sounded so fussed, he tried so hard to be a masterful husband, that instead of weeping Anne turned aside, covered her face with her hands and burst into laughter. Harry turned crimson. He struggled with his dignity and lost, and he was the one who went stamping out of the hall.

'Well by morning?' Piers repeated Anne's assurance. 'That's certain?'

'As certain as anything else about her.' And having won her point with Harry, Anne frowned at Piers and said again, even more fiercely, 'No thanks to you!'

Piers did not answer, perhaps disappointing her. She went off with her head in the air to find Harry and make her peace with him.

'She was teasing, I bluv,' Richard said. He felt very oppressed and strange. He looked closely at Piers as he flung himself on the settle in an exhausted fashion, closing his eyes. The logs burning on the hearth made great lights and shadows, but it seemed to Richard that they cast only shadows over Piers. Richard sat down by his brother as he had done that morning, waiting for him to open his eyes and speak.

'It would be easier if we knew her name,' Piers said at last.

He sounded very weary—like an old man, Richard thought. And from thinking that the girl herself might be bewitched, Richard admitted that if there was a spell at all it was more likely laid on Piers. His heart thumped uncomfortably, again with that feeling of being excluded, a feeling of coming loss that he wondered how he would bear.

'Then what would you think her name might be?' Richard asked. It was a foolish question and got no answer, so Richard tried again. 'One day her kin'll come seeking her and she can go safe away.'

Piers smiled faintly and something burst in Richard.

'Nothing's bin the same since you bring her here!' he cried. 'Oh why did you never come to Harry's wedding— poor Sola had to die anyways. Think—if you'd stood with the rest of us to see 'em wed, you never would've known Brother Hilary had asked for you. Think on that!'

'I have thought.'

'Only this forenoon you wanted her gone—'

'Stop badgering, minnow,' Piers said. He yawned, more with sickness than weariness, but a sickness of the spirit which would not be relieved as his physical sickness

had been last night at Mantlemass. The pair of them, he
and Richard, sat nagging each at his own worry. The logs
burned bright and brighter, then shifted and began to
fall in ash. Now both brothers were silent, their silly
bickering had died away; but nothing better had come
to take its place.

Richard did not go away to school that spring, for the
handing over of the Priory had unsettled everything;
there was a harsh, boisterous element abroad that was
hard to understand. It was Judith who settled the business
by saying they should keep the boy near home. So it was
arranged that he should go each day to Mantlemass,
where the manor secretary, Austin Woodward, was to
supervise his studies. He was a thin, dry man, but handsome—there was some pleasure to be had in observing
him across the table top. He was a clever man, too, but
he had a reedy voice. Richard used to watch his voice,
riding up and down in his throat like a frog in a bottle
and never finding its true home in the hollow of his chest.
It was true that by this arrangement Richard was denied
the new comrades he had hoped to make, but still he had
the familiar pleasure of racing up and down the track
between the two households twice daily, seeing the
season change. Also, since his grandmother was strict
about formal manners, such as the seating at table, the
order of serving and so on, he learnt prudence in such
matters. Again, he was much petted by Dame Cecily's
companion, old Jess Truley, who gave him sweetmeats
and cakes to eat on his way home. After he had been at
lessons two months or more, and at dinner each morning
with the Mallorys, he found himself on comfortable
bantering terms with his cousin Susannah. Because she
was the youngest member of the household she held a
privileged position and enjoyed it. Richard moaned to
her when lessons went badly and she told him rudely he
was an ignorant lout.

'I'd learn twice as fast, come Master Secretary had the teaching of me,' she boasted.

'Girls need not be taught lessons,' Richard answered, not sure whether he was boasting back or speaking enviously.

'There you have a nice point, Richard,' his grandmother said from her place at the head of the table. 'None were taught to me, and at fifteen years old I had not the brain of a sparrow. Lord, what a silly thing I was till my aunt taught me how to read! I saw to it my daughter need never appear such a fool as I had until then.'

'Now, mother,' said Master Simon Mallory, 'we have spoken of this and ended the matter.'

'Young girls have plenty to fill their days, without book learning,' said his wife, in her prim little voice.

'I never was a good housewife, Mary,' Dame Cecily announced. She swallowed the last bite from her platter and leant back in her chair. Her voice had taken on that note which made it clear that she had not much love for her daughter-in-law. 'But no better husband could have come my way.'

'I did not mean,' began Mistress Mary, very flustered— then plumped her hands down together in her lap and closed her mouth hard.

'Madam, I pray you—be a little kinder,' Simon Mallory said to his mother, though there was laughter in his voice, however much he tried to disguise it. 'You will always tease and rebuke poor Mary if you may.'

'Mary rebukes me,' Dame Cecily retorted, 'for she knows well that your sister was taught just as you were, and profited from it. And she, too, got a fine husband— as their son Richard will tell you.'

'Aye, madam,' cried Richard, eagerly nodding, not only for his father's sake but because he greatly enjoyed these mild family bickerings, from which his grandmother always emerged easily triumphant.

'Well, Susannah,' Dame Cecily said, 'what do you say

about it? Shall you marry a man content with an ignorant wife? And what of your sisters? Margaret—Elizabeth—are you happy to stay witless?'

'Mother, mother,' murmured Simon, shaking his head at her, 'let be.'

'They have not answered, Simon. Speak, my dears.'

'Thank you, grandmother,' whispered Margaret, standing up in her place and bobbing, 'I am not clever enough to do lessons like Richard.'

'And I am not clever enough, neither,' said Elizabeth, though at least her voice was louder.

'Well, I'd best learn cleverness if I've none already,' said Susannah, 'for I shall marry Richard.'

Richard could hardly wait to get home to tell all this to Piers. He made a good story of it, feigning the voices of the little girls, sitting bolt upright and pulling down the corners of his mouth to ape his aunt, and scowling darkly in the part of her husband.

'Susannah's like to be hard pressed to marry her cousin,' Piers said, grinning at Richard's performance. 'The Holy Father must give dispensation for such unions—and here in England now it seems we must all forget the Pope. So says King Henry. All else is treason and heresy and I know not what besides. Best tell Susannah so and save her great disappointment!'

'She'll never leave her hold of me, brother. And if there's no Pope, then who's to say us Nay?'

'Be a patient suitor, then,' Piers advised him with a grin. 'The whole world can go to-and-agin I dunnamany times afore you come to wedlock.'

'I wish it might do so afore Susannah come to lessons,' Richard said rather gloomily. 'She always get what she want. It's for ever Yes to Susannah from our grandmother.'

He was right about that, for his youngest cousin did indeed join him across the table from Master Secretary. Since she was so sharp and quick, Richard was bound to work twice as hard. Yet she was a companion he began to enjoy, and as the days lengthened, moving into spring, she would come half the way home with him along the track when lessons were done. Though he often treated her scornfully, for his pride's sake, she was always ready to strike back. He respected her for it. She comforted him for something he knew too surely he had lost—not his brother's love, certainly not that—but very certainly his full, unstinted attention. That, now, he knew he must share.

On a day in March Harry and Piers rode in to the town on business for their father. Harry was to see the sadler, Hayler; none stitched harness as well as this man, and his removal to his father-in-law's business was constantly bemoaned at Ghylls Hatch. Piers was to inspect a stallion recently brought from France by a merchant of the town, and already sire to many fine progeny. Master Medley might have come with them, but he was gone to Mantlemass to discuss various matters of joint concern. The farming of both lands was managed by Simon Mallory but there were always labour questions to be decided, possible arguments about fencing, which fields should be marled and how the grain store stood now at the end of one season and the beginning of another. Anyway, Piers was by now acknowledged to be an even better horse manager than his father. Many such tasks as today's went to him without any question, and he greatly enjoyed them. They had enormous bound pedigree books at Ghylls Hatch which it was Piers's pride to know by heart. The books had been started years ago by Dom Thomas's godfather, Roger Orlebar, who in his turn had inherited the stud from his father. That March morning Piers was riding the black mare, Dignity, whose great-great-grandsire had been sired by Ebony, most valued of all Ghylls Hatch horses to date, the favourite mount until his death of Piers's grandfather, Lewis Mallory. Harry was riding a great raking chestnut called Russet, whose looks were bound to impress, if not to alarm, though his

temper was mild as milk. Harry liked to ride Russet, most
of all for his height. Harry was not a tall man, though he
was handsome.

The day was fine and quiet, the land hesitating on the
brink of the early spring, as if fearing to be gulled. There
was the inevitable farming worry going on, as to whether
it were good to get ahead, or whether late frosts would
come to undo that good. A pale sun shone in a lightly
misted sky and the air was utterly quiet except for a great
rising of larks. The weather had been dry for several
weeks, so the road was fairly firm. The brothers rode
steadily, and though Harry sometimes shouted a sentence
or two over his shoulder, Piers was silent. Ordinarily it
would have been the other way about, but Harry's
marriage had made him more forthcoming, while Piers
had lately taken to being silent for whole days at a time.
He might almost have been deliberately trying to put
himself into the thoughts and feelings of one who would
not speak—though in fact they were all of them beginning
to fear that the girl who had become absorbed into the
household was not obstinate but dumb. She had been
made so, perhaps, by the shock of Dom Thomas's murder
allied to whatever unknown terrors had beset her before
that—she could only have been carried off by the two
horsemen, that was certain, for she had cried for help.
But it began to look as if the how and the why of all this
would remain a mystery. There was a new priest now
at Staglye, and when he came to visit at Ghylls Hatch,
or to act as chaplain at Mantlemass, as his predecessor
had done, he spoke to her long and patiently, but at the
end of it he had only been able to shake his head. He was
Father Oswald, and he was one of the new sort, accepting
reforms, but cautious and kind. It was said that the priest
who had vanished had been taken up for heresy and was
imprisoned, but none knew for sure if this was so.

At the foot of the downs was the river running through
marshes that were water-logged at this end of the year.
A careful way had to be picked down to the river's

crossing. Above, the town stood on its hill, the old decaying castle at its summit. It was hard to believe the place had ever withstood sieges and housed great lords. The walls gaped where time had crumbled them and townsfolk in need of building material had picked what they wanted and trundled it away. In the same way, on the edges of the old road running towards the town in more or less decay all the way from London, there were gaping holes and pits where the hard core beneath ruts and weeds had been dug out for use elsewhere. The castle stones were old enough, but the base of the road was far older, laid down, so Dom Thomas had once told his nephews, by the Romans who ruled England perhaps a thousand years back. And certainly when men dug for building stuff they sometimes turned up broken weapons and pots and even gold coins—so perhaps Dom Thomas had known what he was talking about; Harry at the time had told Piers he considered the idea a bit fanciful . . .

'We're not the only ones going in to town,' Harry shouted, surprised to see so many both riding and walking in the same direction. Though the season was advancing, there could not be much marketing yet, so the numbers did seem unusual.

'Maybe the sun bring 'em out,' Piers said. For here it was shining more brightly, the thin mist was drawn back from a sky most wonderfully blue. As they came nearer to the town it seemed that something more than common daily trading was afoot. There were knots of people, both riders and walkers, talking together at crossways, and many others hurrying with an almost frantic urgency.

'Is there a fair, master?' Piers asked, pulling up alongside a respectable looking man in a fine leather jerkin, with his wife riding behind him.

The man looked at him sombrely, said 'No,' and kicked up his horse.

'Whatever else,' Harry said, 'it don't look to be a friendly feast.'

The brothers rode on, neither admitting to a feeling of

unease. As they approached near the east gate, the river behind them now, they could see a crowd, of boys or apprentices by the looks of them, pelting through the gate, shouting as they went and making that kind of rumpus that causes quieter folk either to step back cautiously or to shake a threatening fist. Today no one either hindered or shouted abuse, for the general tide was all in the same direction.

'What's that they shout, Piers?'

What they heard was like a chant, but they could not make out the words. They reined in to listen, the horses a shade bothered and shifting restlessly.

'The Priory,' Harry said. 'They say over and over *The Priory, the Priory.*'

'We'll never get our business done today, Harry. Best leave the horses at the tavern and let our boots carry us.'

'Aye,' agreed Harry. 'That were best.'

Yet both hesitated. Their curiosity was a leaden curiosity. They more than half knew what they were going to see, and dreaded it, but had to be sure.

The tavern was locked and shuttered, as if the landlord feared a riot. He was watching from his top window how the crowd thickened towards the Priory, and he saw the brothers and shouted that they should come in by the back way. The Medleys always baited their horses here when they were in town, and the landlord would not have thought to deny good customers. He came down at once, opened the door and took over Dignity and Russet.

'Mind your way, masters,' he said. 'We niver yet see a day like this'n.'

'What like is it?' Piers asked cautiously.

'An ugly, scaddle day, to my thought. Though they say it were sure to come.'

'Is it the Priory?'

'What else? You know well how it stood empty since the brothers left—and where they find lewth now, poor souls, is any's guess. But two day behind yesterday—there's others come.'

'What others?'

'King's men.'

Neither Harry nor Piers spoke, waiting for what the landlord might say next, knowing already what must come.

'Hacking it down,' the landlord said. 'Battering it, sirs. They come through the place at dusk. My old 'ooman shruck to see 'em, for she has a feeling for such things— she knew why they was come. Then yesterday, early noon, it get about, and this forenoon, as you see, masters, a great crowd go running to squinney at the work.'

'We'd best go squinney, too,' Piers said. 'See the horses safe till we get back.'

The Priory of St Pancras stood below the town, at the head of the valley and with access to the river traffic. Its huge cluster of buildings had grown over the centuries until it was of itself a citadel. Its great church reared tall as a cathedral. Five hundred years had gone to its making. Thousands of men had built and adorned it out of love and piety. For miles in the countryside around lay farms and pastures administered by its community, paying tithe to the Prior, ordered by him to the profit of the establishment. The influence of such a place could only be enormous. The sick and the poor, the pilgrim and the traveller from abroad relied on this place for shelter, care and hospitality.

Today the people converging on the Priory of St Pancras were not going to learn of the monks, or beg, or seek food and shelter; they were not seeking healing and care, nor were they setting out to hear mass or sing vespers in the church, nor to make their confessions, nor to see their sons and daughters married according to the rites of the Church. They had come instead to witness an execution, to see the place destroyed.

Harry and Piers shoved through the press, sometimes let pass, sometimes shoved in turn and elbowed, and sometimes shouted at by louts not usually so bold.

'It's certain we'll be parted,' Harry yelled over the

tumult. 'If be, I'll look for you at the tavern. By'r Lady, it's ugly here.'

They pushed on until they came where a crowd of men seemed to guard an entry. It was a gaping entry, for there the Priory wall was down and looked as if a giant had taken a great bite at it with teeth as big as boulders. On either side, where the wall still held, men and boys had scrambled to the top and perched there, many laughing and jeering, cheering the work on with loud rough cries of encouragement. Others straddled the wall in silence, their faces blank at what they saw. Some had pulled off their caps and clung there bareheaded and pale. Many women staring through the broken wall cried and wailed and called on Almighty God to witness and avenge this horror. And there were others, both men and women, who wept silently as they watched.

'It's as he said,' Piers muttered. 'Dom Thomas said it—*There shall not be left a stone upon a stone.*' He looked around for Harry, but he had moved further along the wall. A great hammering and battering made Piers look up, as many others were doing. Five or six men were scrambling along the ridge of the roof over the great nave of the church, working away fiercely and keenly, dragging and tearing, peeling away the lead in great strips and casting it to their fellows below. And each time a strip of lead reached the ground a cheer went up from the workmen on both levels. There were others within the church itself, for suddenly there was a great shattering of glass, and through the broken windows came stools and benches as if winged, but losing their wings and crashing and splintering as they hit the ground.

Instantly, the crowd divided in more than mere opinion. It split into watchers and doers. The rollicking young lads and those who had already cheered on the despoilers, now surged through the gap in the wall and snatched up stones to throw at windows yet unbroken. Those among the watchers who had stood, not gloating silently, but ashamed to speak, gave a great groan and rose up in fury, brandishing sticks and anything handy, even drawing knives and rushing forward like an army. A terrible noise of conflict broke out as the two factions met and struggled and heads were broken. And all the time there was the thin deathly sound of glass breaking into fragments, always, it seemed, one more and yet one more, continuing like the high scream of a madman with nothing left to destroy but himself.

In the confusion, Piers made his way through the gap in the wall. Ahead of him a group of men holding plans or papers of instruction, consulted together earnestly, indifferent to the noise within or without. With wide sweeping gestures they pointed out this or that, nodding together in a satisfied manner. They looked tidy, upright citizens, yet they, most certainly, were in charge of this work. They seemed mostly young men; indeed as Piers stared at them, thinking of his uncle who had given years of his life to this place for the honour and glory of God, he saw that one of the men was his own friend, Robin Halacre.

He called out 'Robin! Robin Halacre!' and went slowly towards him.

'Piers! I am glad to see you—indeed I am!' Robin was smiling and clasping Piers warmly by the hand. 'Did you think me still in Oxford? You look quite *shoke*,' he said, giving the word a good country sound, as if recalling a quaint saying he had all but forgotten.

'Then—you've left the university?'

'I have found more urgent work, as you see.' Robin's pleasant fair complexion showed no tinge of shame or sorrow, rather he looked spry and well-fed and pleased with himself. 'I am fortunate to have a friend in the nephew of the Vicar General himself. Master Thomas Cromwell,' he explained kindly. 'It is he who orders and controls all this. So I have found good employment and am very glad of it. I have been a hungry student too long.'

Piers could find nothing to say. He remembered how

bold and fine Robin had seemed, with his talk of corruption and the holocaust to come, of reform and new ways in a new world.

'Come now, I'll show you how it goes, Piers. But best take off that hang-dog look. I'll have my masters saying I keep strange friends.'

'Your masters are not my masters,' Piers said. 'Nor your friends mine, I reckon.'

'That's sharpish talk,' said Robin, his smile dying. 'Mind your tongue, you fool. You know I wish you nothing but good—but mind your tongue. These are not trifling days, I can tell you. *Mind your tongue!*'

'He died in good time,' muttered Piers.

'Who? Who died in good time?'

'My uncle who was Master of Novices here.'

'Forget him,' Robin said roughly. Then he smiled at Piers again ingratiatingly, 'I must get back to my work.'

But Piers had already moved away, swept up and carried along with the rest, buffeted and pushed from all sides. From the churchyard where many paused to hack at the gravestones, he saw numbers scramble through broken windows or wrenched doors into the cloister and so through the whole complex structure of dorter and guest house, sanatorium and kitchen.

And in the kitchen a great throng chose to stay. What the monks had left behind was soon dragged out—sacks of meal and flour, butter salted in crocks, great jars of honey. The urge for destruction was like a fever spreading. They began to slit the sacks, to smash the crocks, to tip up the jars of honey, watching it gleefully as it spread slow and sticky across the floor, so that those running in later slipped and fell and rolled in the mess to howls of delighted derision. Then some more cunning moved swiftly into the cellars, breaking open butts of ale and wine and drinking as if they had not swallowed a draught in their lives before. They were no longer able to help themselves; they were possessed. As Piers, struggling to escape, braced himself at last against the door of the

Chapter House, he saw men dragging the carved stalls into the centre of the floor and setting light to them. He saw men and boys dancing and spitting and relieving themselves against the doors and walls. Soon, he thought, sickened by it, only a shell would stand as sole testimony to the skill and the piety of centuries that had been offered, perhaps too proudly, to the honour and glory of God.

Harry and Piers rode home even more silently than they had come. No business had been done—the saddlers' had been shuttered and bolted and none knew where the merchant was whose stallion Piers had come to inspect. The brothers had stayed longer in the town than intended, first finding one another, then arguing whether to attempt to find their men, then being thwarted in that purpose. It would be dark long before they reached home and the way seemed long and dreary, sped by nothing but the most distressed and melancholy thoughts. Harry, not an imaginative man, was telling himself he would never go near that place again. Townsmen, he decided, were of a different breed from the foresters he knew—they were foxes to the forest stags, jackals to the lions he had proudly moved among when he was in London—and they were not for him. He'd stay safe at home all the rest of his days, he told himself. He would keep Anne and what children they might have safe in the forest. They had plenty of land, the horses brought a good return— and they might strike into other ways of making a fair living.

They were walking the horses up the steep hill three miles or so south of the forest pale, and Harry spoke for the first time since they had left the town behind them.

'They say there's iron on the platt next Withy Wood,' he said.

'What of it?' Piers asked, jolted out of his pre-occupation.

'Could be time we take new ways.'

'Take new land, too,' Piers said, 'if you mean to start a furnace blowing. We'd need a licence for Withy Wood, likely—and ask me we'd not get it. Too much hue and cry over timber taking already. And too many turning to smelting, what's more.'

'War takes weapons. There's always war. How long afore we start fighting in France again?'

'I'd sooner keep the trees, Harry. Sooner horses, anyways. What's wrong wi' horses so sudden?'

'Maybe it needn't be Withy Wood,' Harry said thoughtfully. 'There's other ground looks promising. Plashet's Piece for one. That's Mantlemass land, my father tell me once.'

'It's where he was born,' Piers said.

'Who was?'

'Father. There was a dwelling there, so he say. Well—you know all that, Harry.'

'I never knew precisely where,' Harry said slowly. 'I know his parents did live out of wedlock—that I do know and don't much like. Still, none I can name ever make any fluster over it.'

'If any knew, they've forgot. He call himself Master Medley and naught besides, but I never heard it called to account. He never speak his father's name, or his grandfather's. Did he to you ever—being the eldest son?'

Harry shook his head and Piers said what he had often thought—that if there was a secret, then it was most likely to die when their father died.

This exchange had slowed the brothers more than intended. Now they became aware of the increasing dark and pressed hard over the last mile or so. They clattered into the yard and all the dogs broke into a clamour. A lad ran out to take the horses. Piers and Harry were barely out of the saddle before Richard appeared. He was carrying a lantern, and as he held it up the light fell on his face.

'Now what's so pleased the little brother?' Harry cried, mocking. 'How he do smile!'

'Piers!' cried Richard, ignoring Harry. 'I found out something you want to know, surelye.'

'Have you so? That's good. There's none inside'll get pleasure from what we've to tell.'

Richard's face fell. 'What?'

'Later. Tell your news first.'

Richard stood there grinning again and seeming unable to start.

'Spit it out, minnow!'

'Her name's Isabella,' Richard said.

7

Isabella

In the hall the girl was sitting on a stool by the hearth
with Judith on one side and Anne on the other.
Master Medley stood by and at least four of the maids
peered and whispered excitedly in the background. She
sat with her hands palm uppermost in her lap, a gesture
at once defeated and generous. Her cheeks were flushed,
she bit her lip yet smiled as she did so. When she looked
up at the three brothers entering, her eyes glittered.

Anne sprang up when she heard the door. She ran
forward, seizing Piers by the hand and crying 'She has a
name! Your stranger has a name!'

When she said *Your stranger* Richard looked up at
Piers and saw what he had expected. A key already fitted
into a secret lock had turned a little further; it had turned
away from Richard and towards the girl. He had known
certainly for the past three months that this must happen
and must be endured. It was his misfortune that it came
sooner rather than later, and harder still that he himself
had urged it to a climax.

'What else?' asked Piers, very still.

'Be patient! Nothing yet,' Anne said. But if she had answered *She told us she is the Queen of Fairyland*, the effect could have been no greater.

Richard said quickly, not wanting Anne to get in first, 'Come and greet her—come and call her by her name!' He tugged at his brother's arm, and Piers looked at him quickly and keenly, and then away—back to the girl. 'Isabella, she is called,' Richard insisted, as if Piers might not have understood.

'It was Richard found out,' Judith said. 'She spoke to Richard. All this time and no word—and then suddenly she spoke to Richard.'

'He was greatly set upon it,' their father said, laughing quietly, pleased with the boy's patience and success. 'He try every name he know—from Anna to Zillah, you might say.'

'Not the first time, neither,' Richard said. 'I never thought of Isabella till today. When I come to it first time, she toss up her head like a yearling. So then I go right away back to Elizabeth, and on to Mary and Maud, and back to Eleanor. Then I come again to Isabella. A marvel come about! Up she sprang, brother, and cried out loud "Isabella!" '

'She said "I am Isabella",' Anne gabbled, snatching the tale from Richard, 'and then she span like a puffball and fell in a faint.'

'She fell so I feared she must have died,' said Judith. 'Very particular, she look. And us-all went to-and-about to fetch her back to life. Then up she sat. "Isabella?" I say to her. And she say, "Aye. Isabella," and fetched a great sigh. We must all kneel and give thanks, for it's as like as nowhow to one let back from the grave.'

It was only then that Piers came to himself. He moved the last few steps, shaking off Richard, though gently, crouching down by the girl and staring into her face.

At last he said, 'Tell me.'

'I am Isabella,' she said. 'Isabella . . . Isabella . . .' Soft from disuse, her voice was as frail as feathers.

She should not be badgered or questioned, Master Medley pronounced. Father Oswald, sent for to see and speak with her, said the same. He said her soul was bruised by something they could not know about, any of them.

'Those bruises are best not probed. Her eyes are clear. Sometimes God sees fit to blot out things too painful to be recalled. His mercy shall heal her. We must trust to His wisdom and our own for anything more.' He sounded very positive and reassuring and all of them listening nodded and murmured in agreement. 'No questions, then, remember. Let her say what she may wish to say. No more.'

But they could none of them do other than treat her as one who had returned from some far and dangerous place—for a time they seemed to guard her, as if they feared she might return to that place. It was pleasant to see how everyone smiled at her and helped her, consoling and patient when she sought for words or stammered in their utterance. They had always been kind, but mostly because of Dom Thomas, because she seemed a sacred trust from him to them—from him to Piers who had stood at that moment to answer for all the family. Sometimes it had been a struggle to be patient, she had seemed such a poor, bedevilled thing. Only Piers had failed, shouting abuse and driving her to flight. Had she forgotten that along with the rest? Had she indeed been given a fresh start in life, everything up to yesterday or a few days before quite wiped away and to be forgotten for ever? They sometimes talked together quietly when she was not there, about her family, wondering if she were mourned. There was nothing whatever to connect her with any other living being in the whole world—she had carried no possessions, she wore no jewel, no locket, say, that might have borne a crest to be deciphered. Her clothes had been plain to the point of poverty, quite apart from the mess of mud and blood on her outer garments. Yet her bearing, her gentle and withdrawn manner, her skin grown delicate as she recovered her health, spoke of some decent upbringing. Also she began now to display many skills. As she became more and more a part of the household she joined in the housewifely activities of Judith and Anne—and never needed instruction. She could bake, brew and sew. She could read. At Mantlemass one day she took up Dame Cecily's own lute and plucked it with easy familiarity. She did not speak a great deal, hardly at all unless addressed directly. She never joined in general talk but sat listening, sometimes smiling, sometimes nodding. But having in some inexplicable way come to a point of change and of renewal, she seemed content with what her discovered name had given her— an identity of her own. As the spring advanced and the earth grew warm and there was much activity, digging and sowing of summer crops, she took a spade one day and by herself dug a small bed of earth, tucking up her skirt to do so, kicking off her shoes, confusing them all by presenting a quite different Isabella with other skills to offer. She went about the forest seeking diligently, and came back with seed heads of one kind or another, in which the seeds no longer rattled but had begun already to stir and uncoil. These she planted in the newly worked earth.

'What will come of them?' Judith asked her.

'They will grow!'

'But what are they? And will they have fine flowers?'

'They are to make possets. Potions for sickness. Tinctures.'

'What are they called?' insisted Judith, unable to resist testing her as far as this.

'I forget,' said Isabella.

Soon she seemed to dislike these words and softened them to 'That was before,' 'That was long ago.'

In the months after the violence of the Priory's destruction the countryside seemed quiet, the forest looking inward about its own concerns. News from further afield was less comfortable. It was said that there were many shut away in the town gaols, both men and women, taken on heresy charges but not yet tried. Defensively, when these tales went round, no one was ever named. Sometimes it happened that a man might disappear from the forest community without making any open farewells, but none knew if he had been taken by authority when he was beyond the pale, or whether he had feared such a happening and forestalled it. There were always strangers about, casual labour at hay-making and harvest, workers in furnace and forge who stayed a month or two or six, and then moved on. Harry, pursuing that sudden idea of his about working the local iron ore, and riding about on a tour of inspection from one furnace to another, came home astounded at the numbers now employed in the growing trade. This year it did seem that there were more than usual moving about the forest, picking up a day's labour here or there. Some of these might well be secularised monks, accepting the return to the world; such men had many skills to offer, the lay brothers particularly being accustomed to working on the land, to building and brewing and caring for animals. It was not in the nature of the forest people, however, to ask questions of strangers. The forest had always been a place of refuge, for the lawless as for the persecuted, and by long tradition such people were accepted and often permanently absorbed.

Richard came home from lessons at Mantlemass and he, too, had a tale of newcomers.

'Goody Truley's sister and her husband,' he said.

'I never hear Jess Truley speak of a sister like to come visiting,' Judith said.

'Well, there she be, mother, large as life. My grandmother give 'em the little steading next the big barn.'

'Staying then, are they? Not just visiting?'

'He's to be steward, grandmother tell me—she say old Walter's past it—providential, she say, another steward coming so pat. His wife's to help Jess and that about the household.'

'What's she like?'

'Squinneys down her nose at me and Susannah, that's what like she is,' Richard replied. 'He's Robert Leethwaite, and her name's Kate.'

'Leethwaite? That's no name from these parts. He'll be from the north, like as not.' This time Judith spoke as if the man could only be a barbarian, and she wondered out loud that Dame Cecily should take in her servants from such wild and distant parts. 'What manner of man is he?'

'Portly, but not tall. Fine grey curly hair. His cheeks go into great creases when he smiles. His voice is a thunder-rumble, but kind.'

'I'd best go calling,' Judith decided. 'I wouldn't want Dame Cecily put upon.'

Richard grinned, for he was quite certain that his grandmother was well able to judge man or woman very soundly—and even if she had lost her cunning in such matters, her son and daughter-in-law would not be gulled. However, Judith could not endure her ignorance of the newcomers and went off that afternoon to Mantlemass.

'Very fine and tip-tongued,' she pronounced of Kate Leethwaite. 'And her goodman of quite a noble manner. But to see Jess! So fussed and flurried as she is—so bothered lest they don't please! It's my guess they've fell on hard times, poor things.'

At this time of year there was little leisure at Ghylls Hatch or Mantlemass. At one time the Mallorys had kept sheep, driving them out to downland pasture at this season. But they had long abandoned all but a small home flock bred up for mutton, and kept cattle instead. These were fattened on rich ground in the wealden country a little to the north, where the Mallorys had acquired another manor through Simon's marriage. Likewise, much of their ground these days was given over to hops, which needed considerable care. In fact there was so much doing that Richard and Susannah were free of lessons for a time. At Ghylls Hatch many mares had foaled successfully, and besides there was young stock due for breaking. Master Medley was out about the stables and the fields at all hours, and Piers and Harry with him—though Harry was by now so besottedly in love with his wife that he could hardly bear to be torn from her side and would dawdle with her all day if he could. Anne would have her first child before Christmas. She and Judith and Isabella sat together in the evenings, stitching and embroidering little shifts and caps. Anne never ceased chattering. She was in such good health and high spirits that Judith was forever trying to calm and steady her.

'You'll have a flighty babe with a head full of down! Do say your prayers quiet and decent, Anne, and ask for a fine sturdy son.'

'I'll have a beauteous daughter, just as soon,' said Anne, yawning and stretching like a lazy cat.

'You must give Harry an heir for Ghylls Hatch.'

'So I will—so I will,' promised Anne, without a doubt about it. 'But I'll have a daughter for myself first.'

Of the three women, Isabella sewed best. With intense concentration, with a head bent and hardly ever raised, she stitched as small as pinheads, made wreaths of leaves and flowers so fine they might have been fairy work. She never tired. She was as industrious and disciplined as a woman three times her age. And how old was she? She could not tell them, but she seemed to be about eighteen. A stillness hung over Isabella, an air of waiting. And indeed as they watched her the others would exchange glances and little smiles, for they waited, too—though not, as might be expected, for her to remember more, to tell them all the past, to know herself at last for whatever she had once been. They waited instead for what Piers might have to say to her, and what she would reply. Perhaps, even, they hoped that she would never recall anything more than her name, but that here she would be able to start a new life quite unattached to anything that had gone before.

For all the months from Christmas when he had struggled to deny her and been defeated, Piers, too, watched Isabella, as she moved about the house. There was such a quiet about her at times that she seemed to be listening for sounds very distantly heard. Then, with her head a little bent, she frowned. It was only at such moments that her serenity was ruffled. Piers longed to know what it was she thought she heard. He almost found himself listening, too, as if he would be able to catch whatever was sounding somewhere in her memory or her imagination. At such times he wondered desperately if there could be some madness in her that might suddenly appear. This was a deep and bitter worry. For if, as now he wished, he should wed with her, and there was indeed some hidden canker in her mind, what children might they have? Sometimes he woke sweating in the dark night and seemed to hear the wild laughter of his crazy sons and daughters echoing along the walls.

A fine summer followed the mild spring. Outside this small world of Medleys and Mallorys the religious changes continued to gather pace. Many supposed miraculous images were discredited and destroyed, shrines pulled down, heretics burnt. In the church at Staglye Master Medley had one day found Father Oswald removing memorial brasses from their places to pack away and hide under a great slab in the crypt. There was a growing wave of destruction of all such presentations of the human form on tombs and monuments—as Dom Thomas had known well there would be, when he rescued the immense brass of Prior Nelond. Father Oswald, by no means out of sympathy with reform, still hoped to save the treasures of his parish church.

'Maybe one day they shall be replaced,' Master Medley said to his household. 'So Father Oswald hopes. But we're told,' he added drily, 'that we must no longer believe in miracles.'

'We believe what God tell us, not what the King decide,' said Judith.

'Keep that for safety in your own thoughts, wife,' he said, 'for that's what they call heresy and treason, both.' Seeing how distressed she looked, he took her hands to comfort her. 'Something better will come of it all, so Father Oswald swear to me. Purer, he say. And some-one-time I think it, too.'

When Isabella's carefully nurtured plants came to flower, she picked some whole and left others to seed again. She worked with the garnering in the still-room, and soon there stood a row of flasks on the shelf, each sealed over with tops made of parchment begged from the Mantlemass secretary when he came to Ghylls Hatch to write up the books of accounting. On each parchment she made some coloured sign that she might know one from the other.

'For you,' she said, pressing a flask into Anne's hands. 'To make strong blood. To help with your labour.'

'Shall I drink it or paint it on my cheeks?' Anne asked, holding the flask up to the light to admire its colour.

'Nay, Anne,' said Isabella, but smiling, 'pray do not tease. And take this also—this shall whiten your hands when summer's over.'

'Can you truly not remember where you learnt so much?' Anne asked.

'It was before,' said Isabella, and turned away. She did so quite calmly. She was in no way flustered by the question.

'Well—thank you for your kind thought,' said Anne. But when she told Harry he looked quite wildly alarmed and ordered her not to touch the stuff.

'How do we know it is not some subtle poison?'

Anne laughed, 'We know Isabella would not give it to me, then.'

'She might not understand what she was doing. That is all I mean. Children make up such cordials for their dolls—of berries and the like. But you would not drink them.'

'Judith knows distilling. She uses roots and berries.

And she learnt from your father's mother, so she said.'

'She, poor soul, suffered for it. Evil persons said she was a witch. She died because of it.'

'Aye—well do not you tell me Isabella is a witch,' said Anne sharply. 'I will leave the stuff—but only for your sake.'

As the spring sowing, so the harvest. It was big and there were hands enough to bring it in. There would be more than enough for their own granaries and that meant some could be sold overseas. Everyone turned into the fields when the time came. Anne, with only two months to go before her confinement, kicked her heels crossly and watched the others working in the sun. Harvest was cheerful toil and she would gladly have joined in. A year ago she would have objected to burning her skin, but happy in her marriage to a countryman she was prepared to share his status and no longer considered Judith's brown complexion coarse. Isabella went into the fields without question, without even being asked, taking her place there as by long custom. Though she was small and light she had much concealed strength. She was set to work gleaning with the other women and the children, but she knew how to use a sickle, how to bind the sheaves and stook them.

'I never see a maid so dainty work so easy, Piers,' his father said to him. 'Look how she seize great sheaves. It's a wonder.'

She looked up and saw them watching her. Her kerchief had fallen back off her head, her feet were planted sturdily, the toes curling to grip the ground as she swung her load. Her arms, bare to the elbow, were as golden from the sun and air as the corn she was gathering up. Seeing them there together, she smiled. There was no longer any reserve in the smile. She stood clasping a sheaf, and called across to them.

'You have no-ought to laugh!' she cried, broad as any harvester in the field. 'I'm no pathery, peaked ooman any more, I reckon.'

It was the most she had ever said, her first words spoken country-wise. How much she must have been listening and absorbing all this time. It pleased Master Medley and roused in Piers such an excess of tenderness that he turned away to hide it.

The sunshine and the harvest freedom and fellowship seemed to work in Isabella like yeast in hops. Her sedateness was forgotten. She began to talk twice as much as ever before, she laughed easily and seemed filled with great inward strength and certainty. Now when there were several there and Piers was among them, it was to Piers she always turned. Each day of that fine season, almost each hour, she seemed to move closer to him, until soon it was taken for granted she should be at his side. Now after the months of watching and whispering they began to say Piers and Isabella, Isabella and Piers—at first significantly, then with smiles, then naturally, as if what happened next was an accepted and a fortunate conclusion.

Each day, so packed with labour and so long, was like a week, a month, a year—until with the last load carried an eternity came to an end.

They kept harvest home at Mantlemass in the big barn there. By a custom going back to the days of Dame Elizabeth FitzEdmund, the men and maids sat bashfully down, while the gentry poured ale and handed platters. Later, the dancing began. Medleys and Mallorys joined in a round or two, then said goodnight. Without them the merriment would run more freely, certainly till midnight.

Dame Cecily led the way back to the house, Father Oswald on one hand, Master Medley on the other. Harry had his arm round Anne's waist to help her along, and she was singing quietly. The little Mallory girls, Elizabeth and Margaret, left their mother to catch at Isabella's hands. Mistress Mary walked alone. Richard and Susannah chattered together as usual, Piers walked with Judith and his uncle Simon. Behind them came some others—Austin Woodward, Jess Truley, the Leethwaites. It was a warm still night, the moon immense. The certainty of work well done glowed in the veins like good wine. As they came into the house Master Medley paused on the threshold to see them all inside, cuffing Richard and making him duck, tweaking Susannah's hair as she ran squealing past, catching Anne by the hand so that she would pause long enough for him to kiss her cheek. He stopped Isabella in her turn.

'None worked better than thee, mistress,' he said. 'So thanks to thee, too, for our good harvest.'

Isabella had looked down modestly as he praised her. When she lifted her head, so much was revealed of her hopes and fears that he in his turn looked away.

'Get you in, now,' he said gently; and stood waiting for the rest.

He checked Piers, as he had checked the others, but then waited until they were alone by the door.

'Sir?' said Piers. He made it a question but he knew what his father was going to speak of. He did not know whether what he said would be welcome. Piers tried to breathe steadily, but his heart thudded painfully in his ears.

'Piers—I see the way your thoughts run—leastways, I do think I see 'em. If not—then I made a great boffle of it.'

'No boffle, father,' Piers answered. 'My thoughts run on Isabella.' He forced himself to say firmly: 'I think we should be wed.'

His father said nothing for a moment. 'If you have courage to wed a mystery,' he said at last, 'then I'll tell you I think so, too.' He looked sharply at Piers. 'Have you courage?'

'I pray so, sir.'

'And I pray so—for I have always the knowledge that you swore to cherish her—and who it was asked the oath.

I know the undertaking was for all of us—and so she may live with all of us at Ghylls Hatch—for my old friend's sake it shall be her home for always. But if this is to be, then as I see it, Piers, you must either take her to wife or go away. So partly it is for my own selfish reasons,' Master Medley said, 'that I can see you must wed. I have three sons—but I cannot spare any.'

'At first I did try to hate her,' Piers said in a low voice. 'I was a churl to her because of it. You know that. Anne called her my stranger, and so she was. And half I wish she could have stayed so. But, sir,' he said, smiling doubtfully at his father, 'it is altogether too late. I am bewitched, perhaps.'

'Most men are bewitched somewhen or other . . . You are as young as I was when I asked for your mother. Too young, her father thought; so we were bound to wait. When she died, I thought of that wasted time and it took me near to despair . . . But there was no mystery in her—as there is in Isabella.'

'Mysteries need not always be solved,' Piers said unguardedly.

'Ah, then,' his father said, 'I see you do fear what could be revealed.'

'Only as it might part us—and once I did wonder if there might be some madness . . .'

'No.' Master Medley sounded very sure. 'There's no madness in her. Look in her eyes—and what do you see?'

Piers smiled a little. 'I see myself.'

'Well, then, as your grandmother would say—God shall mend all. So let that be our prayer.'

'Amen,' Piers muttered.

'I think it should be as soon as she will. And my blessing to you,' his father said.

Piers kept the knowledge of his father's approval and nourished it warmly for some days. He still needed to think about what he certainly wanted most in the world.

He dallied over the business. It gave him pleasure to be with Isabella and to know he might ask her to be his wife and there would be no family hindrance. It was almost impossible to believe that Isabella could give any answer but the right one. Yet deeper than anything he had ever puzzled over, fought to be rid of and overcome, was the most carefully concealed doubt of all. Had she in fact forgotten—or had she decided she would not remember?

'It shall be today,' Piers told himself, as the year tipped over into October days. That evening he went fishing. He had intended to go alone, to calm himself a little. But Richard overtook him as he set out.

'Shall you go to the pool, Piers?'

'Aye, for a while.'

'Shall I come, too?'

It was not what Piers wanted and he said sharply, 'Leave pestering. Am I never to take a step alone?'

Richard stopped in his tracks, and at once Piers was contrite.

'Ah, poor minnow. I'm sad company.'

'You'm busy with other things,' Richard excused him.

'When it comes your turn—remember me . . . Still— not your turn yet—so come on down with me and see what's rising.'

Richard followed Piers gladly, but finding himself snivelling a bit, he hung behind until he should deal with the matter. He hated Piers's preoccupation but he could not even begin to hate its cause. Piers was seven or eight paces ahead of him when they started down the bank to the water. Both at the same moment saw the girl sitting there on the bank. Piers's heart leapt, but Richard's sank like a stone. He turned without a word. He knew that Piers looked back at him briefly, but did not call after him. They must have made a tryst, Richard thought, and that was why Piers had wanted to go alone. At the top of the long bank Richard could not help himself pausing to peer down through the trees. The birches, already gold, shifted in the slight breeze like coins falling magically through the air. Isabella was wearing a bright blue gown that showed starkly among the green and gold, and by the sudden flurry of colour Richard knew that she had leapt to her feet. Then he saw her hand outstretched and saw it caught by his brother's. The blue gown and Piers's brown doublet were so close they might have been one garment.

Richard knew he was spying, whatever kinder word he might prefer to use. He turned away and left the pool, and the lovers, and the first years of his life in a tangle behind him.

8

The Summertime

In May his father made Richard a gift. He seemed to feel that his youngest son was being left out of family events. Anne and Harry now had the 'beauteous daughter' she had wanted so much, born before last Advent, baptised Cecily Anne and soon called Cecilia. Richard was a godfather, but he was more concerned to be named sponsor, in due course, to a child of Isabella's. Since Piers and Isabella had seemed, ever since their marriage last autumn, to live in a world of only two people, Richard wondered if anyone would be told of a coming baby until it was self-evident. So he did feel rather shut out, missing Piers's companionship most bitterly, and finding it strange to be so bereft when he still saw his brother every day. Or did he see only Isabella's husband? Richard moped a bit, sighed over his lessons, quarrelled with Susannah. It was because of such a quarrel that his father was made fully aware of Richard's state of mind. Master Medley found the pair striking and shouting at one another on the way from Mantlemass to Ghylls Hatch.

He rode up behind them and they were so busy hating one another that they heard nothing. He dismounted and grabbed one in either hand. Susannah clawed at his wrist, almost spitting in her fury. Richard, shocked into stillness, stood with his head bent, breathing very hard, his eyes filling with tears of rage and humiliation.

'What have I here in my two hands?' Master Medley demanded. 'A pair of rafty fighting birds? Richard— you're too old to fight with women—you'll beg your cousin's pardon for the sake of courtesy. Though by'r Lady, Susannah Mallory, I think you must do likewise.'

Behind the words, Richard heard his father's smothered laughter.

'Get you to it, Dickory,' he said sternly.

Richard glowered at Susannah, and she glowered back. Neither cared to give in, but as he was the elder, and a gentleman into the bargain, he should do it first. He found this intolerably unfair, but his father had often enough in the past pointed out that life and custom were most often hard on women.

'I beg your pardon, cousin,' he said, half strangled by his reluctance.

'Beg it you may, but I'm not giving any,' snapped Susannah.

'Is it so deep a quarrel?' Master Medley asked. 'So bitter? Enough to part friends? Why what could it be that seem worth such a hurley-bulloo?'

The two contestants looked sharply at one another. There was a long silence, then Susannah said, 'I mis-remember.' She eyed Richard under black brows. 'You tell'm.'

'I misremember, too,' said Richard.

His father laughed, then. He put a hand on the neck of each and gently banged their heads together. This caused Susannah to burst into wild tears, and he let Richard go, that he might swing her up in his arms and kiss and comfort her.

'Now, look'ee, Su,' he said, 'be kind to my son Richard,

for he has much to bear just now. And for me—I've no daughter and only a puling granddaughter too small to play with. So be kind to me, too, maid, that am your loving uncle.'

He set her down again, and she went to Richard meekly and laid her cheek against his. This was too much for him. He pushed her off and stepped back hastily, smearing with distaste at the tears she had left behind on his face. She recovered her spirits at once, kicked his ankle sharply and most painfully, and ran away bawling.

'She'm a goblin, no better!' cried Richard, hopping on one foot to nurse the other.

He walked home at his father's stirrup, polite as any knight's squire, declining to be jossed-up to share the horse, for he was feeling full of injured dignity and threatened manhood. When they reached Ghylls Hatch, Master Medley said he must go to look at the fillies in the field called Headlands, and Richard should go with him. There were four of them, the pick of the three-year-olds and glorious in Richard's eyes. He hung on the gate and watched them, and as his father discussed their points with him as with an equal, the boy's self-confidence returned and he forgot that he and his cousin had kicked and struck at one another like babies.

'Which is the best, think you?' Master Medley asked.

'The bay,' said Richard instantly.

'I think so, too. That's Breeze. She's Zephyr's blood in her, as you know. Let's whistle her up.'

It took a little time for her to honour them, but she came at last, picking up her feet neatly, arching her neck and then lifting her nose and looking at them warily and condescendingly, ready to dance away sideways if they presumed too much.

'Your'n, Dickory,' his father said.

He could not believe it at first. Only after he had ridden her five or six times, and on the seventh when he called her she answered and came running, could he be sure it had happened. He would not forget little Argent, who had carried him bravely, even though this last year he had grown taller and heavier. But here was his first man-sized mount—'Master Richard's mare', he would hear her called by Matthew Ade and the rest of the stable men. In those first summer days of having Breeze for his own, Richard could hardly bear to be separated from her. The gift made up for a great deal. His brothers, too, impressed, gave him some attention; Harry rode out with him twice, and Piers went once. Harry, Richard thought wisely, having been wed a year longer than Piers, had regained a little of his composure and could spare more time. It would be a good thing, in Richard's view, when Piers had been married long enough to be himself again.

But for Piers these summer days were days of magic. He worked hard and well, but he did so less for the work's sake than because when he woke each day and found Isabella beside him he gave thanks for being alive. And although he was still seeking some final solution which was withheld, he felt none the less like a sorcerer who has brought a statue to life, who sees it breathe already and leans towards the day when it will walk and run. He who had laughed at Harry's anxious obsession with Anne in the early days of their marriage, was now himself the victim. Yet he was not teased as Harry had been teased. He would not wonder why. He preferred to accept their tenderness and care of Isabella without admitting they might do so because she remained a mystery. For although she often laughed with him now, and even once ran through the house singing, she was indeed a mysterious being, a woman born into the world fully grown and with many talents—with everything but a past. Sometimes he did try to trip her into some revelation, but either she appeared not to notice, or she became distressed, so that he was quick to comfort her and change the subject.

Piers took his happiness as it came, and in much the same way both households inclined to turn inward upon their own small community, stopping their ears against the outside world. None ever passed through from London, or from the market towns, without some painful tidings or other. The destruction of the shrine of St Thomas at Canterbury had caused an uproar throughout Christendom; the Pope had thundered and threatened. The King had thereupon issued a proclamation that declared the saint had been a rebel against his own King Henry II, and therefore was no more than a traitor justly executed. There was news of more executions, too—of the Abbot of Woburn, of the Prior of Lenton; while side by side with these ecclesiastical alarms came more worldly news, of the execution of those who, by their Yorkist descent, might claim some right to the Crown. Even the old Countess of Salisbury, who might have been a rallying point for revolution, was imprisoned and threatened with death. Her son, Henry, had been executed already.

'We are best where we are these days—as ever,' Master Medley told his household. And Harry no longer complained that they lived like peasants—he could be glad of it.

Of them all, Dame Cecily tried the most diligently to understand the changes in church affairs. She spent long hours in discussion with Father Oswald. He had brought to the chapel at Mantlemass the copy of the Bible in English, which had been ordered by the Vicar General to be kept in every parish church. The parishioners of Staglye had been hostile and the priest wished to keep the huge book safely until he could persuade them to reason. Meanwhile, to read aloud from it gave him such joy that all the household was expected to assemble at each midday to hear him . . It was the best of the new ways, Dame Cecily said.

In the high summer, Piers was working a young horse on open ground in the higher parts of the forest. He saw a horseman passing on a track below him, and recognised him at once, in spite of distance and some change of appearance. He wheeled his young gelding and turned to head off the traveller. When he came within distance he shouted out, 'Hi, Robin! Robin Halacre!'

Robin checked at once and waited for him. He sat very still, and his horse, a far better one than he had ever ridden in the past, tossed its head against the flies and stamped in the hot afternoon.

'Are you bound for Ghylls Hatch, Robin? I hope so. We've not met for I dunnamany months.'

'We met last at the Priory, I think,' Robin said. His tone reminded Piers that they had disagreed. 'And I am in a mind to visit Mantlemass, not Ghylls Hatch. Are you well? I'm told you are wed.'

'So I am.'

'But none could tell me who she is.'

'Wish me joy, then,' said Piers.

'I do. With all my heart, and you know it. Does she come from hereabouts?'

'No,' said Piers. 'I thank you for your wishes—though I had to ask for 'em!'

Robin laughed and said he would have come to it of himself, given time. When he laughed he was more recognisable. Otherwise he was exceedingly well decked-out—sprugged up, Piers might have called it, if only to take him down a bit, for his manner was austerely self-confident. He wore his hair short, in the new style.

'Come home with me and let my wife welcome you,' Piers said. 'High time you married, too, friend.'

'I have work to do. I am much from home. I have lodgings in London now. You will recall I am employed by the Vicar General himself.'

'Oh aye—that's not forgotten,' Piers said, his spirits beginning to sink at his old friend's pompous manner. 'Well—come another day. Have you been to see your parents?'

'Indeed. I like to see them decently settled. It is the least I owe them. And then, as I said, I have this business at Mantlemass.'

'Business? I judged it to be a friendly call.'

'Friendly, of course, Piers. A word with your good

grandmother, no more. I understood a Robert Leethwaite had taken up work there.'

'Well?'

'He'd be a very competent and most excellent steward. He is steward at Mantlemass, I am informed.'

'Yes,' Piers answered shortly. 'A good steward, as you say. An honest sort of man.'

'Let us pray. You did not know, I daresay, that he was a monk of Cartmel—a Carthusian priory in Lancashire. An unfrocked monk, you see—I was not certain if Dame Cecily knew of this. You shall tell me and save me a journey. We are well met.'

'Unfrocked is one thing,' Piers said, keeping his surprise to himself. 'Returned to the world without much choice is quite other.'

'There is always a choice—there has been a choice until lately,' Robin corrected himself. 'Leethwaite is pensioned, if others are not. But we'll say returned to the world, if you prefer. A secularised monk, to be particular.'

'My grandmother'll know, for sure. She always know such things.'

'I sought him by instruction, Piers. It was said that— like you—he had married.'

'Should he not? Must he be in the world—and keep his vows?'

'He is absolved of his vows—you know that, I am certain, and are tormenting me. We must try to agree, Piers Medley. We have known one another so long.' He smiled, again looking his old self, but too briefly. The smile went out like a snuffed candle, leaving the same bleakness behind. 'He may not marry a nun, however.'

'Well, I suppose not—if she be a nun. But nuns have come back to the world, too. I'd expect they should seek out their own sort.' Piers kept a blank face, but began to wonder about Kate Leethwaite.

'In the world or out of it,' Robin explained with exaggerated patience, 'nuns have taken a vow of chastity and may not wed.'

'They are released from their vows—you said so.'

'The monks, yes. And the nuns are released from the vows of poverty and obedience. The vow of chastity remains binding.'

'Well, God save all!' cried Piers. 'How shall a woman of no fortune live chaste in the world? She's bound to find protection.'

'Her family, no doubt, will shelter her.'

'Many of these women come from humble homes. How shall they be supported? Ask me, Robin Halacre, there's no absolution from the vow of poverty, neither!'

Robin sighed deeply. 'You are an old friend, but old friends must learn new ways. This nun we are speaking of should not have entered a convent in the first place—I told you years ago they are sinks of evil.'

'Men's minds are sinks of evil!' Piers said hotly.

'This is mere cant, Piers. Now tell me before I lose my temper—does your grandmother know this man Leethwaite is a religious?'

'She never spoke of it. But I tell you—she always know such things.'

'Well, if his wife be of the same persuasion they must be put apart—they shall be divorced.'

'Divorce come quite the thing, these times,' said Piers. 'Goody Leethwaite's a perfect decent body, sister to my grandmother's old companion. So you may guess at how long she bin known at Mantlemass.'

'Keep your ears and eyes open, then. Truly I'm pressed for time—I'd be glad to ride straight on. Well—I shall expect to hear from you.'

'If there's aught to tell.'

Robin was getting angry, and Piers knew it. He longed to goad him still further, but saw the folly. Far better to part before Robin started sniffing round that last ambiguous remark about Kate being 'known at Mantlemass'. It was a perfect half truth.

'We never quarrelled till now, Robin. So let's make an end.'

'I've no quarrel with you. But you'll lose that tongue of yours and the head it wags in—if you don't suit your manners to the time. We part friends. Only do you remember all I've said.'

'I'll remember, surelye,' Piers answered.

Robin kicked up his beautiful horse, with a jingle of spurs and bit, and a creak of good leather. He wheeled away and did not once look back or raise his hand in farewell. Piers sat his now fidgeting young mount and stared thoughtfully after Robin until the trees took and hid him. He sat there thinking about the Leethwaites, remembering his rather stately manner, recalling her piety. Of all the cruelties he could think of, this that threatened them if Robin should be right, did seem the most bitter. He wondered whether or not he should speak of the matter to his grandmother. It was true that she usually knew everything about those she was concerned with, but if it should be otherwise, then he would rather not burden her. It seemed better to keep Robin at bay if necessary by giving him occasional news of the pair. He would not care if he had to think up lies. He absolved himself of that sin before it was committed.

Through the summer and on into early autumn, Piers was on the watch for Robin, but never saw him. He decided to let things rest. He was ready with his stories should Robin suddenly call him to account.

The harvest that year was disappointing—easily a third less than the previous year. Also the Mallorys lost some cattle, driven away from the grazing grounds by a thieving herdsman. It proved, said Harry, that they must all have more strings to their bow, and he insisted that his idea of going into the business of iron founding was a sound one. 'If the King go on his way there'll be war with France soon enough—next year, or the next. There's always a market for gunstones.' Master Medley had agreed that the matter might deserve some consideration;

but he was uneasy about the timber situation. For years back there had been complaints about the quantities taken for charcoal to keep the furnaces going. The number of furnaces increased all the time and the fuel would surely run out and cause ruin and distress to those who had plied the trade. No one would deny that iron was being used for more and more purposes, or that new methods and improvements might be on the way—but it was certain that houses and ships needed timber, too, and it was being filched from one industry to feed another.

What with the situation in the world, the poor harvest and consequent lack of feed for the animals, the endless and sometimes furious arguments between Harry and the rest, a certain gloom was cast over both households. Christmas helped them on, and once into February the promise of spring took over and they were themselves again. Then it was Easter, there was the fair at Lewes and Piers took Isabella riding pillion. Richard had waited for an invitation to go too, and Piers had known that but turned a deaf ear to hints. Richard was growing resigned to the changes that life was bound to bring. He was leaving his childhood behind, which made him at once more aggressive and more sympathetic. He had suddenly discovered the pleasures of learning, and Austin Woodward had said he should be sent to the university. There was much discussion about this—indeed as Piers rode with Isabella to the fair he was speaking about his brother.

'If he go to Oxford,' Piers said, 'he'll change. Like some other I know. He seem to me meant for our way of living—the horses and the land. Come Harry truly get himself licensed to sell iron, then there's a whole mortatious lot more to be thought on. Could be he'd need Richard to work for him somewhat.' He waited for Isabella to speak, but she did not. Sometimes she did seem to slip back almost into her old silence, and it troubled him. 'How do you think about it, love?'

'What? What did you say?'

'Are you dozing, back there?'

'Thinking.'

'Of Richard?'

'Nay, not Richard. Of you, husband.'

'Ha!' said Piers, and heard her laugh, very light and faint behind him.

'Tell me more of the fair, Piers.'

'Why, 'tis for livestock and people, both. The sheep with four legs you shall see matched by the sheep wi' two.'

'And there shall be many stalls, with goods for selling. It was Anne told me.'

'Have you never—' he began; then as usual after that involuntary opening he changed the sentence. 'Have you never thought a new gown might not come amiss?'

'I have thought that!'

'Then we shall buy cloth, my girl. And you and Judith and Anne shall stitch it. Afore we jog home we'll buy a fairing for Judith and one for Anne.'

'And for Richard, also.'

'Well—maybe. But Richard's not the dawlin any more.'

'The dawlin?'

'The littlest. The littlest pig of the litter. The infant of the house. That's Cecilia's station.'

'For the time,' said Isabella.

'Aye—for the time,' he answered.

After that she was silent again, and soon they drew near the town. Today, as on that March day that seemed so long ago, the town was crowded with people on the move, but with a blessedly different purpose. Today the noise and bustle was all concerned with trade, with bargaining, with the back-slapping pleasure of meeting friends and choosing fairings. The crush was immense, and with the bleating of numberless confused sheep, the cries of buyers and sellers, the shouts and squeals of children thrusting and shoving and running among the crowd, with bells ringing, dogs barking, quacks crying their wares and a pageant being played on a cart in one corner of the market-place, it was hard for any man to hear his wife or his neighbour when they spoke to him.

Isabella clung to Piers's arm, she seemed confused and a little frightened. He had thought vaguely that he would do some business about hides while he was there, leaving his wife to gaze among the stalls. But he saw that he could not leave her to look after herself, even in that friendly crowd. Harry should have brought Anne, and she could have looked after Isabella. Harry had had other things to do, and Anne had woken sneezing—which had set Judith diligently dosing her—a sneeze might be nothing but dust inhaled from old rushes, but it could be the plague itself. Judith always concluded it might be the plague and went to work vigorously, so purging and posseting that it sometimes seemed a wonder the patient survived either way. 'She need only feverfew,' Isabella had said. Judith had never quite accepted Isabella's skill with herbs, and had preferred to go her own way . . .

So now Piers had to escort Isabella along the rows of stalls, and point out this or that, buy her comfits, gape at the sword-swallower; watch boys hurl clods and rotten apples at a man in the stocks and feel her shrink and shiver.

'What has he done?'

'Nothing so very wicked, reckon. A vagabond, maybe— a beggar. They'll whip him out of town later and he'll be glad to go.'

She pulled at his arm, tugging him away, and he was not sorry to go. They found a weaver's stall, and there long swags of cloth were hung, of all colours and all textures. Isabella gasped at such riches, like a child at a peepshow. He watched her wide eyes and flushed cheeks and he suddenly felt sick with ignorance of too much. He loved her deeply and dearly, but he was still seeking the true Isabella, she was still his stranger.

At the weaver's stall Piers saw Robin Halacre buying a roll of honest country cloth that he might well have been expected nowadays to despise.

'Good-day, friend,' Piers said, putting his hand on Robin's shoulder. 'That's suent cloth you chose.'

'I'll tell you which to choose, Piers,' Robin answered, unsurprised by the meeting, so that Piers had the impression he had been noticed already in some other part of the fair. 'I know good work when I see it. Halacres are weavers four generations back, as well you know.'

'My grandmother tell me once how a Halacre wove and dyed her first country gown,' Piers said, glad of Robin's openness, of the fact that he was still willing to acknowledge humble forest origins. But then his master, and his master's master, the late great Cardinal, were both men of simple birth.

'What else does your grandmother tell you?' Robin asked.

'Naun you'd need to hear—or you'd know of it b'now,' Piers answered easily. 'Did'n' I say I'd tell aught there were to tell?' He drew Isabella forward. 'Here's my good wife, Robin, who has heard tell of you.'

'I have wanted to greet you, mistress,' Robin Halacre said. 'It may be late in the day to wish you joy—but so I do.'

Isabella flushed and paled and flushed again, giving him her hand and a modest curtsey, thanking him in a small voice.

'Are you long in these parts, Robin?' Piers asked.

'Long enough for a certain load of business. Our gaols are stuffed full of heretics and the like. They must be brought to trial. I am sent to set the thing in motion. One way or another, the prisons must be emptied—though I daresay only to fill again. These are treasonable times, alas. My master, you may know, is now made Earl of Essex.'

'You are grown a power in the land,' Piers told him, half grim, half mocking.

'Barely,' Robin answered, so humbly that he sounded arrogant beyond words. If not yet, he seemed to say, then soon . . .

He left them. Isabella chose a crimson cloth and Piers paid for it after some cheerful haggling. Then they bought laces and ribbon for Anne, gingerbread and marchpane for Judith, and some dry sticks of cinnamon she had asked them to look for. The cinnamon was sold by a wizened brown man from some distant place, and he had also nutmegs, of which they bought a handful. Piers chose a hunting knife for Richard, its handle made of a polished tine from an antler—then said Harry must go whistle for a gift, for there was no more money to spend.

They rode home slowly through a fine clear evening, the spoils of the day stuffed into a basket that Isabella carried over her arm as she sat behind Piers once more; and once more silent. They crossed the river with many others making for home. Then gradually the crowd thinned and by the time they were at the outskirts of the forest, among few trees and small farms worked by freehold tenants of one manor or another, there was no one following, no one ahead. As they came upon a bare upland, the open stretches of the forest, set between groves and hangers, took the declining sun until all the atmosphere bounded and pulsed with colour.

'Sleeping again?' Piers asked Isabella.

'I am thinking. Just as before.'

'Even of the same thing?'

'Aye—a little more, a little less.'

'Well, I was not told then—so tell me now.'

'I said it was of you I thought. And so it was and so it is—in part.'

'Who learnt you to tease?' he asked. 'Tell me.'

'Promise to tell no other.'

'Why—yes, if you wish. I'll promise.'

'Then—I think it will be autumn.'

'What will be autumn?'

'October . . .' Her voice was fainter than it had been when she started to speak, but then she cried quite desperately, 'You *know* what I would say! You *know*! But I cannot—I cannot say the words.'

Now he was silent himself, and after a time she pressed against him as she sat there on the pillion, and said as he had said—'Sleeping?'

'No!'

'Then—tell me what I am trying to tell you.'

'I think it must be the dawlin,' he said.

'Aye, Piers—the littlest pig—the infant of the house . . .
That was what you said.'

Piers reined in, and slewed in his saddle so that he
could look at Isabella over his shoulder.

'Is it true?'

'True.'

'It maze me,' he said, grinning.

'But it never mislike you, husband, surelye!'

'How foresty you speak,' he said.

'It'll be a foresty child, that's why.' She laughed, and
it was a pleasant sound. 'But remember your promise,
now. Don't tell! Don't tell! Not yet.'

As they rode on, he felt a strangeness inside his mind.
It was the leaping of life from point to point that bemused
him. The present was forever being snatched into the
past, the future into the present. All that had seemed
eternal was sliding fast into another eternity. Perhaps until
this moment when he became aware of renewal, Piers had
never believed his days could end. He knew it then as he
had never known it among all the prayers and the
promises of heaven or hell. He, too, would die, and the
forest would grow over the place where he had been.

When they reached home, Piers dismounted, then
lifted Isabella down and held her tenderly. He did not
speak, but she seemed content with what she saw in his
face. She took his hand and led him to the house.

When they went indoors everyone ran to hear about the
day and receive their fairings. Anne was better, the baby
had cut a tooth, the fire leapt on the hearth and all
seemed hopeful and good.

'We met Robin Halacre,' Piers said.

'Oh, grown very grand, they say,' cried Judith. 'And
much good may his grandness do him, the way he gain it.
He better've stayed a forester. What did you think of him,
Isabella?'

She did not answer for so long that Judith repeated the question.

'What did you think of Piers's friend Robin, child?'

'I feared him,' Isabella said.

9

The Rising Wind

Harry had spent a great while trying to persuade his father that the time might have come for them to set up in iron. That year a commission was working for some months over the whole forest area, assessing land, water, timber, game, that a report might be made for the King, who was the land's lord. At one time there was a rumour that His Grace was to come hunting, setting up tents among the ruins of the old palace of King Edward II. Nothing came of the project, which disappointed some and relieved others. The repercussions from a royal hunt would have been loud and many, and in Master Medley's view the idea should be left to slumber until it was forgotten. Dame Cecily had been greatly put out by the rumour. Because of the circumstances of her aunt Elizabeth FitzEdmund's marriage, Mantlemass was held directly from the Crown. Dame Cecily had envisaged the tents collapsing in wind and rain and the whole entourage descending to find quarters with her—an honour, she said, she would be richer without. Perhaps the King was

too preoccupied to follow up the idea of the hunt, for it
was said he was to marry again, a princess from the Low
Countries whose name no one seemed to know. It was the
incidence of the commission that brought about the
rumour of a royal hunt, and it was the meeting of free-
holders and others to discuss the resulting matters of
business, that gave Harry the lever that he needed. He
and his father spoke during that time to men they barely
saw at any other, and there was much talk and exchange
of forest information. The profits to be gained from iron
were as much discussed as the market in bloodstock. A
neighbour from some miles away, who had set up his
furnace where years ago an attempt had failed to drive a
hammer by water power, was happy to deliver an opinion
on the relative merits of Withy Wood and Plashets Piece.
Master Medley said it should be Plashets or none, for
Withy Wood was too near home. He had no desire or
intention of making his days and nights hideous with
the inevitable clangour. Eventually—and it was months
later—Harry and his father went to London, to consult
on the legal side of the business. Master Medley was still
not altogether won, but he was bending increasingly to
Harry's keen persuasion.

There was a great movement of deer about the forest.
The incidence of strangers, riding blindly along tracks
they did not know, constantly losing themselves and
thrashing about in the undergrowth, had disturbed the
herds, who began to shift their grounds. They broke into
Ghylls Hatch land, destroying the fences in several
places, and damaging good coppice; coming so near the
house, too, that they trampled Isabella's herb garden and
ate the tops off Anne's rose trees, that her father had
given her when she first left home. It was a bad time to
put men to the repairing of fences, since the hay crop
was early after a warm wet spring, and a couple of fields
were ready for cutting. Piers threw tools and stakes into
a cart and set off to do the job himself.

'Mind you come home my way from lessons,' he

ordered Richard. 'I'll be down Harthide bottom mostly all day, I reckon. I'll need a hand later, so don't go doddling about the place wi' Susannah. Set out smartly, and no maundering.'

By the time the day was ending Richard did not even want to hang about. So much had happened that he could not find Piers fast enough. He arrived breathless, and poured out in a burst of excited gabbling a tale that sent Piers's heart down into his boots.

'You heard all this? You saw it? Now swear you're not making a tale of it?'

'I am not! I tell you, I were there!'

'Had they left when you came away? Which track?'

'They'd gone a bare minute. Come quick up Platty Bank and you'll see 'em yet—they'll be taking the turn down by Goodales, most like.'

Piers threw down his mallet and began to run, Richard at his heels. They scrambled over a thorn hedge and made for rising ground on the far side of a stone outcrop. When they reached the top, breathless, a small party was coming into view below them to the south-east, proceeding from Mantlemass to pick up the road into the town. A man rode on ahead of four or five others, two of whom wore the livery of the town guard. Behind one of these a woman rode pillion, and after all came a man running and shouting. But the horses, though they went at a sober enough trot, covered the ground a good deal faster than he could, and gradually he dropped behind. Then he stood looking after them, trying to get his breath, and at last fell on his knees and bowed his head, beating at his forehead with his clenched hands.

'It's him,' Richard said. 'Robert Leethwaite.'

'Oh God,' said Piers, sick with pity. 'God save them both!'

'He was a monk!' Richard cried. 'A monk of Cartmel—that's north somewheres. They shut the priory down and some of his fellows got hanged. He was lucky. Then he met with some others turned out—some nuns with 'em—and Goody Kate was one. She was going to her sister—

Jess, I mean—so they got married and she brought him, too. But she was a nun, Piers—a true professed nun! So they must not marry and Robin Halacre came with four others and took her away.'

Piers groaned. He could have warned them. Why in God's name had he not done so? How could he have been so simple as to think that Robin, grown cunning in cunning service, would not smell out what he wanted to?

'They're to be divorced,' Richard rushed on. 'Piers, are you listening? He can go where he list but they must never speak to one another again, not without there's four others present—not on pain of fine and bitter punishment. That's what your friend Robin Halacre tell—he read it off a great paper.'

'My *friend*! Did he say where he take her?'

'To Lewes gaol. Till they get the Bishop to hear the case. What do you think of it?'

'I think men make out God's cruel and pitiless—but it's them that's both. Oh may I be forgiven, minnow—I knew what Robin thought! I didn't bluv enough of it. I could have saved 'em!'

Richard was sobered by his brother's distress. 'Reckon it's too late now,' he said. 'But, Piers, I did think our grandmother might catch that Halacre by the throat and shake him till he rattled! She look fearsome.'

Piers was no longer listening. He had started off down the bank, leaping and striding, his fair hair rising and falling with the movement, so that he looked as if he were flying. Richard stood to watch him go pelting on and watched him reach Leethwaite's side and drop down beside him. He watched Piers take the man by his shoulders and speak to him urgently. At last they both rose, Leethwaite very tottering, catching at Piers to steady himself, obviously crying and sobbing in his distress, so that Richard looked away. The excitement had gone out of the business. He felt very low spirited. He knew Piers would help Leethwaite back to Mantlemass, so he himself returned to where the cart was standing by the battered paling. He picked up a mallet and made a few half-hearted strokes at the stake Piers had been working on when he was interrupted. Then he threw the mallet down, altogether disgruntled. He almost wished he had kept the story to himself, for he had been looking forward to Piers's company as they worked together on the fence.

After a time, as Piers did not return, Richard decided to go home. He wondered what to do about the cart, and concluded it had better stay where it was; Piers would surely return, if not to finish the job, at least to collect his pick and mallet. Richard contented himself with moving the horse and tethering him on fresh ground, then turned his back and started for Ghylls Hatch, the horse whinnying after him.

Isabella was standing outside the house when Richard reached it, shading her eyes against the afternoon sun, and gazing out over the forest, as always anxious for Piers to return. She was looking very sturdy now, the baby being due in four months or so. It had been she, not Piers, who asked Richard to stand sponsor to the child, and this had greatly pleased and flattered him. 'Only be sure it is a boy,' he said loftily, 'for I have already a goddaughter and would sooner not have two.' Isabella saw him coming now and opened her mouth—but he anticipated her words and cried out in a little high voice— 'Oh Richard, where is Piers?'

'Well—where?' she demanded.

'Just now he go to Mantlemass. There's great doings there,' Richard said, settling to the delights of a fresh audience, pouring out his story with more drama even than before, for now it had acquired an extra chapter. Isabella's response could not have been more satisfactory. Her eyes went dark with horror, she turned pale as milk. He half expected her to faint.

'Where is he now?'

'Where's who? Robin—Leethwaite?'

'Piers! Where's Piers?'

'I tell you. He walked Robert Leethwaite home. And justly so, for he looked very particular.' She moved forward swiftly, but he caught her arm. 'You go too mighty fast. He'll come back by Harthide bottom—so meet him there, come you must. The cart's there and the rest.'

She made some sound and flung away and began to run. 'Take care!' he shouted after her. 'Mind my godson, do!' He meant to make her laugh, but he doubted if she heard him. Long before she was out of sight she was calling 'Piers! Piers!' Her voice drifted back to Richard thin and threadlike among trees and shrub. He kicked at the mounting-block alongside the pump as he passed, muttering 'The silly mawkin!' and knowing very well he should not have startled her so, not just now when Judith kept telling them all to treat her carefully. Doubly deserted, angry with himself into the bargain, he went to find Judith, who loved him enough to listen to any story of his to its bitter end. And certainly she proved the best audience of the three, for she did not interrupt, except to repeat the most impressive bits to herself in awe, crying out at intervals 'Lord save us!' and 'What horrors to hear!' and 'Poor souls, poor souls—how should it be their doing?' So that he forgot his worry over Isabella.

'Did you know Jess Truley had a sister was a nun?' he asked her.

'Aye—but I supposed this must be another. I feared to ask for the nun, Dickory, for fear of some sad tale. For so it goes.'

Matthew Ade came to the door then. There was a man come to the stables with a horse that had cast a shoe, and could he leave it till morning?

'It's some o' them about the forest matters,' Matthew told Judith. 'The rest's waiting on him. Should I lend him a nag, madam?'

'I'll see him,' said Judith . . .

By evening, Piers had not come home, nor Isabella. Richard knew Piers would try to get the fencing done before nightfall, and half of him wanted to go and help, and the other half felt dignified and miffed at being deserted. When it was dark, he had still not returned, but there was a clear full moon, quite light enough to work by. But Judith and Anne began to fuss about Isabella. At last Judith sent Richard packing to Harthide and told him at least to fetch Isabella back indoors, for though it was June the evening had chilled, and she must not take cold.

Richard took fifteen minutes or so, running, to reach the place, but Piers was not there. No one was there. The job was not finished, either, though the tools had vanished, along with the horse and cart. Alarm sprang up in Richard's mind, and he thought guiltily of how he had startled Isabella with his story. He should have had more thought and good sense. It was a wretched tale to tell with so much excitement and must have seemed doubly so to a woman so far advanced in her pregnancy—Judith had warned him that some such grew very fanciful at those times, and made great mysteries and terrors out of mere phantoms. It was very quiet, the moonlight seemed to thicken everything it fell on, turning rocks and trees to marble and blotting the ground below them with purple shadows. Then fox and owl cried, the one seeming to answer the other. A chill crept on Richard's spine and his doubts became forebodings. What if he had shocked Isabella into a miscarriage—he knew such things could happen. He imagined how Piers might have helped her into the cart, and driven off to Mantlemass. But he checked on that. Why Mantlemass, when home was just as near? Perhaps because the way to Mantlemass was easier and smoother, safer for a woman in such a state . . . Terrible distress filled Richard at the picture he had conjured up for himself. He stood in the white moonlight, not knowing which way to turn.

When Piers returned to Harthide bottom after leaving Robert Leethwaite at Mantlemass, Isabella was waiting for him. She saw him the instant he came over the brow of the bank, and began to run towards him. Then she stopped. She held out her arms—then let them fall emptily to her sides. He came on down the bank, knowing already as he looked at her one half of what she would tell him. When he came near enough to see her face, then he knew all the rest. As if a great book had opened at the centre and displayed a score of secrets undeciphered, the past seemed laid before him in every particular—all that he had held clamped hard to the back and bottom of his mind, all that he had feared and dreaded and defied. Now it was he who flung out his arms, and she moved in a stumbling way towards him, and fell against him, far beyond weeping.

'I know,' he said at once. 'No one has told me. I see it in your face. I know now. I know.'

'Must I go?' she asked, her voice quite thin and high, as he had never heard it. 'Shall you send me away?'

'If you go, I go,' he said. 'If you die, I die. That's the whole sum of it.'

'Ah, Piers, Piers . . .' she said. She shivered, her teeth chattered. 'I have to tell you now.'

There was an old cloak rolled up in the cart, and some rough wool blankets used for the horses. Piers put the cloak round Isabella, and spread a blanket on a mound of dead dry bracken that he had cleared away earlier to see where to drive his fencing stakes. He pulled Isabella down beside him and held her head against his shoulder, saying finally, 'Tell what you must. If you rather—tell me nothing. It shall all be the same, surelye.'

She began to speak, muffled against his shoulder, making many false starts: 'When I was come to fourteen year . . .' 'When my birthday come, and it should've been my fourteenth . . .' 'My father had five daughters and I was the last . . .'

Then she sat up, away from him and looking at her hands, and except to help her now and then, he did not interrupt.

'It was always known, when I was fourteen, I should go to the Sisters of St Martha. It was a small house, and it was by Horsham, where my home was—only some miles by, and not easy come to. They kept the Carmelite rule a little less in some ways, and more in others—which was what bring it to ruin in the end, I'd say.' She paused, still looking at her hands, and seemed to be gathering her memories together for him.

'And—?' he said.

'And I told you—my father had five daughters and never a son. There was not enough money for portions all round, that was sure. He was in a small way of business. A haberdasher.'

'Even the convent would ask a dowry . . .'

'My two aunts were there. So they took me for my linen and the chest it was packed in—that was my mother's dower chest. With leather bindings and brass locks and handles. And I know you will ask was this what I wanted? I can only tell you it was a known thing since I was five or six year old. Decided when I was born, perhaps. My mother died then. I never thought any other. It was known; I knew it and everyone. I never expected otherly . . . Then my eldest sister was wed, and all the others one by one, till there was none to keep house for my father. So he took a new wife. That year I was thirteen, and it was my birthday. That day my father's wife said for my greater happiness I should go to the sisters then, and not wait a whole more year. She and my father took me that day, that birthday. The Mother Superior praised my father for giving two sisters and a daughter to the Church. She said I was fully young, but in two years I might start my novitiate, and until then I was but a humble postulant, she said, and could leave should I wish. Though she knew I would not wish, she said. And indeed, Piers,' said Isabella, 'where should I go?'

'Your two good aunts were there—they helped you,' Piers said hopefully.

'Aye, one was kind. But one was stern. When any prayed, she prayed longer; when any meditated, she meditated to the edge of death. She was on her knees, for sure, twice as long as any in the community. She was blind, poor soul, and needed to be guided, and so it fell to me to be with her always, on my knees or off them.'

'You were such a child—and they so old.'

'Yes, they were old. They were all old, it seemed to me. It cannot have been so in fact, but it seemed so But perhaps I was never a child. I was an infant—and then I was a postulant. And then I was a novice, as I had been promised. I gave up my hair and took my first vows and wore the habit that novices wear. My father and his wife came that day to the convent, but after that I never saw them again. I was entirely in the community. I learnt to read and to write and to sing. I learnt to sew and to bake, and to distill. And as all worked in the fields and the garden, so did I. And for recreation I was allowed to play the lute. So there was nothing I could not do that any other girl of my age could do.'

'You could not dance,' he said. 'I could have known from that. Had I wanted.'

All this time that she was speaking, Isabella had remained calm, her voice small and clear. Now she began to shudder and to weep, holding in such harsh sobs that he feared she would make herself ill.

'You must not fear,' he urged her. 'I have you safe and so it shall remain. Take care—take care for all of us. You know we shall never be parted.'

'So Kate Leethwaite thought—that she was safe here in the forest with her sister, and with Dame Cecily's protection. But they will be parted—so how shall it be with us? You must think me so false and lying, but it all began to seem a dream—it seemed as I wanted it to. And I rested in that. All the months I was silent, I was struggling to know what should be done. It was not difficult to stay silent—I was accustomed to it. At the convent I learnt silence like a lesson. I cheated myself and I never stopped to think I cheated you. How shall I ever be forgiven—here or hereafter? I shall be punished and so will you, because of me.'

Piers did not know how to comfort or convince her. Though he spoke so reasonably he was deeply shaken, he was chilled to the soul. The immensity of the difficulties that could be ahead for them seemed enough to press him deep into the earth. He almost groaned aloud, but kept his despair to himself for her sake.

'I'll tell the rest,' she said, taking a deep breath and steadying herself.

'Another time. Come home now.'

She shook her head. 'I must tell it,' she insisted, twisting her hands tightly together. 'How the convent was shut down—I'll tell that.'

When the commission first came from the King, she told him, there had been a dreadful flurry and fear throughout the community of women. Some rumour of what might be coming had already reached them. Now the Mother Superior was instructed in the facts of the matter—how it had been decided that there were too many such small houses about the country, and that for all the best reasons, of common sense, of economy, of religion itself, it was decided that many should be closed and merged with larger communities. Grave accusations had been laid against such houses as theirs, she was told, so for the sake of all concerned, in their own best interests, an enquiry must be made. Then the commissioners began questioning the nuns, in twos and threes, in ones, which was most terrifying to them. Suggestions so grave and vile were made that the older nuns trembled and could barely find strength for a denial, while some who were younger broke down into tears of confusion and hysterical fear of what might come next. Then the commissioners, gathering up their papers, went away. But nothing was the same after they left. The sisters avoided one another's confidences and even their prayers seemed to them to be suddenly tainted with heretical lapses. Many were reduced to a state near despair, while others became quarrelsome and vindictive and blamed their superior for what had happened. After some time they learnt that the house was indeed to be closed. The Mother Superior, the Mistress of Novices and two others were offered the choice of joining another house, a Carmelite convent in the north, or taking a pension and returning to the world. Three moved to the north, one accepted the pension, no fewer than three of the old nuns died between the arrival of the commissioners and the result of their report. That left Isabella and three middle-aged women. They must all fend for themselves, which meant returning to their families.

'Two did this,' Isabella said. 'Sister Agnes, who had been twenty years a nun, had no one left of her relations. So she came with me. But she took sick after a few miles, and a farmer's wife gave her lodging. So then I went on. I had a little money the Mother Superior gave me before she left. She could not help more—the revenues of the convent were forfeit. The money was left of my aunts' dowries, and both now had died.'

Isabella set out for home, walking alone in the world for the first time in five long years. It was a bleak and dismal day, and when she came to her own village it all looked different—there were more houses, a new market hall. She did find her father's house, but the woman who lived there now told her that he had gone to London three years ago, and where he should be sought she could not say. 'Best be off,' the woman told her. 'If you're out of the convent, if that be true—then get off and away. We know what sort you are—we've heard enough. There's a mortacious lot of such as you, men and women alike, and we want none of you here, that's sure.' So she asked the way to London and began, in great fear, to trudge along the road in the dank November weather.

'What else should I do, Piers? I could think of nothing—nothing. I slept under a hedge and it was bitter. In the morning when I woke—there were two men watching me. The men you saw. They'd set me Londonwards, they said. They had a miserable pack horse, and they put me up on that. I could not have run away if I would—I was stiff with cold and hunger. As I was lifted on the horse the coins sounded in my pocket, and they took those. After a time I knew by their winks and nods what else they would take. My thoughts were like ice in my mind, but I prayed and prayed for help. I saw by the milestones we were journeying away from London. I think I was half dead with fear . . . Then at the church gate, suddenly out of that dreadful fog, I saw men and horses—your uncle, Piers—and I called out to him . . . And then it all happened as you know.'

She leant back against his shoulder and closed her eyes, exhausted by her own memories. 'Surelye,' she said, her voice full of bitter tears, 'God never could have brought us two together from so far apart—only to damn us?'

Damnation seemed to Piers a good deal further away than many other difficulties, though he was shocked to find the thought so quickly in his mind. He did not believe they could be so deserted in their need, either by God or man. As she spoke of his uncle, some glimmer of comfort came to him. What had she said to him? he asked, in those few moments they were together, before chaos came to swallow them.

'Where I had come from. Who—what I was.'

'And so he answered—'

'He said: Hold it secret, my daughter, till all seem safe. When he said *my daughter*, I knew he was a priest. I did as he told me in the only way I knew—in silence. And then it did seem safe, because you were there, and you'd stopped hating.'

'There,' he said, holding her warmly, 'you have told it and it's done. Now come home, love. There's a tidy shatter o' news to get through, with Judith and the rest.'

'Not home!' Isabella cried, pushing him away. 'Not to Ghylls Hatch! Robin Halacre'll come there and take me away.'

'How should he? You were not a professed nun. You

were only a novice. That's the difference in you and Kate.'

'I took the vows, like any other. They'd be renewed later—made perpetual and binding until death—that's final profession, as you should know. At the end, the Bishop's chaplain came and gave us the Bishop's absolution from the vows of poverty and obedience.'

This time Piers did groan aloud, for he knew what came next because of what Robin had told him.

'We knew we must live chaste,' she said, 'for that absolution was not given. And now—look where I sit with my husband beside me and a child only waiting to be born!'

'Come home!' Piers said harshly. 'I'll protect you, and my father and brothers shall do so, and my grandmother who is as strong as any, and my uncle of Mantlemass— and Robin Halacre shall not dare raise a hand agin you. And if Father Oswald cannot absolve your vow, then we'll seek the bishop. And if not the bishop, then as God judges me, we'll go overseas and not stop till we come to the Holy Father himself. And he shall listen.'

'Shall he?' she asked, her eyes filling again. 'Shall he, Piers?'

'Well, if not, then trust in God. Both us shall do that. But come home now, for all our sakes.'

She said again: 'No. We must go far away. Away from Robin Halacre.'

He heard the frenzy coming back into her voice and she stiffened as he held her.

'We'll think again in the morning.'

'Now. We must think now. Oh I see how it must be!' she cried wildly. 'I must go alone!'

He laughed and said it was already agreed that wherever they went they must go together. 'And that's no more than our marriage vow.'

'Break one, break all!' cried Isabella.

He began to be infected by her fear. He had swallowed the horror of the tale; all its implications in the way of faith and teaching he had accepted; but now, seeing her so frantic, he began to shake in horror at the thought of what could happen to her. It was only with the greatest difficulty that he prevented a glance over his shoulder, as if their enemies had already crept up on them and waited to carry them away. It was this almost childish fear that helped him to recover some kind of calm.

'Wait till morning,' he said again. 'Trust me.' He looked at her closely. It was as though many years of her life had gone over her in the last hour and would not come again. For the first time he saw her as she must truly be, and to be loved not less, but more. 'Now do you lift up your chin a bit, Isabella,' he urged her. 'I say we shall go home.'

He drove the cart back slowly towards Ghylls Hatch. The afternoon sun was now going, but the light was very clear and pierced by the song of thrushes. After the steepish sides of Harthide Bottom they travelled on a high plateau, with Mantlemass standing at its eastern end. The trees being in full leaf there was no visible sign of the house at this distance, while Ghylls Hatch, away to the north-west, was concealed, house, stables, farm, fields and all by the swoop and scoop of the high banks that were its southernmost boundary. They seemed, therefore, to have the forest to themselves, and to be at peace after the turmoils of the last hours, and before whatever new turmoils were to come. From this ground, in spite of the view being blocked behind and ahead, it was possible to see clear over the trees to the open heathland, with beyond it the downs. On the nearer forest nothing stirred as the day slipped into its decline. And then there was some movement in the middle foreground.

Piers checked the horse and turned its head sharply to the left, driving the cart into the shelter of a small copse. He could still see, by standing up on the boards, a small string of riders passing—three, no four of them, one a trooper carrying a pike at rest, and last of all a man with a lame horse. He seemed at the moment that Piers saw him to become aware of the lameness, and he dismounted.

He shouted something to the next in line, and he wheeled and came in his turn to inspect the horse. The two men discussed the matter, while their fellows went ahead, then at last the rider of the lame animal was left to walk and lead the creature on.

'There!' cried Isabella, shrill yet whispering. 'They are come already!'

She made as if to scramble from the cart, but he caught her wrist and held her.

'Wait, now—wait!' he said, for she struggled wildly. 'Hush, while I think.'

He tried to muster some sort of sense out of it all. He did not think the cavalcade appeared to be on very urgent business. The party might merely be one of strangers passing through the forest on the way to the London road. In that case they were likely to have a guide with them, and he could not see anyone he knew. Then perhaps they were concerned with the forest commission and so could be safely dismissed. With all his heart Piers longed for the safety of his own home and people. Once back at Ghylls Hatch Isabella would surely grow calm. And yet he saw with appalling clarity that she had come to the brink of such despair as might drive her out of her wits. She was whimpering and clawing at his hand, trying still to get away.

'You are to trust me,' he said gently, putting his arm round her. He held her against his shoulder and gradually she grew quiet.

Piers knew then that he had come to a moment of time in which his life had to change direction. He had been one of many, young enough to take orders and to expect counsel. He had now to rely upon himself, making his own decisions in defence of his own wife, his own child. He must depend altogether on his own resources.

Having made his decision he stayed waiting as the party of riders moved without haste on its way and at last vanished altogether. Then he shook up his horse, pulled its head into the north-east, and drove off.

10

A Different Country

Isabella looked at Piers in silence as he changed course, and he smiled at her to encourage her. He needed some encouragement himself. Having faced his responsibilities he was now overwhelmed by them. He wished he had been able to speak to his grandmother before setting out for another country—different in many physical ways from the one he knew, but most of all different in being faced alone. The tension went out of Isabella as he smiled at her and she was utterly calm. Her trust in him was pretty well unbearable, for he felt as he turned away from home exceedingly little confidence in himself. He took a narrow track among tall trees, the cart lurching and rattling, so that he felt some anxiety for Isabella. That almost made him laugh—for it was a pretty droll turn of fortune that sent a man into exile with a wife five months pregnant with her first child. Happily there was a place of shelter he could take her for that night.

Once free of the Mantlemass boundaries, Piers drove east and a little north, rising up over those far bare heights of open forest that stretched in an arc of scrub and heather between areas of trees. Up there, where the forest reached its end, thinning into small steadings and pasture lands, there was a farm that had been manor property for many years—a squat, scattery place of outbuildings and walls, where often the sheep had been folded at lambing time, in the days before Simon Mallory exchanged his flocks for herds of cattle. Many oak trees had seeded in that part, but because of the height and the wind that it caught, the trees were stunted and blown, less than a quarter of the height they should have achieved long ago. Young oak was called locally *tillow*, which gave the place its name of Tillow Holt. The place was untenanted at present, but it was kept in care by a mild-mannered, slightly witless fellow named Davy. Davy what, Davy who, Piers had never known, for as in the case of his own father, Davy owned only his baptismal name. His wife and children had been called by it—Goody Sukey Davy, Ned Davy, Jenny Davy and the rest. Goody Sukey had died long ago, the sons and daughters had married and gone away. Davy kept Tillow Holt in fair order on his own, which was all that was asked of him. As a child, Piers knew vaguely, he had had some part in the affairs of Dame Cecily and Master Lewis, and no Mallory would ever see him starve.

By the time Piers and Isabella, driving cautiously, came to Tillow Holt, the moon was up. No dog barked as they approached the farm; there was no sign of life whatever. Davy, unless he had suddenly changed his ways, would be out poaching. Piers hoped he might be, and coming home soon, for he needed food for both of them. Isabella said she was not hungry, but she looked pale and faint.

In the barn there was plenty of straw, rather broken and dusty, but good enough—a welcome sight, too, after the poor harvest of last autumn, which would have left most barns bare by now. Piers settled Isabella there, telling her to rest. Then he unhitched and watered the horse and turned it to pasture. After that he went to the house. He found a good pitcher of milk, half a loaf and some powerful goat's milk cheese that Davy must have made for himself. He was moving off with these spoils when Davy returned. Piers saw him, black against the moon, climbing the stile a hundred yards away. He wore a dreadful old hood pulled low over his forehead and carried a promising bag on his shoulders. His dog was at his heels. He stopped dead when he saw Piers and looked as if he might bolt; but he checked when he heard his name called.

'Davy! I need your help.'

'Master P-p-piers, is it?' Davy stuttered, plucking off his hood. 'I niver see you this nearly two-year, sir. W-w-w-what help, master?'

'My wife's sheltering in the barn. We're set to travel Kent way—to visit with her mother,' Piers said, thinking that he must remember to tell Isabella so. 'Halfway, I stuck a wheel in stoach, so we'm late on our way. I pray that make no matter to you?'

'Hem-a-bit, sir,' grinned Davy. 'You'll n-n-need a bite, dessay. Supper's in my ole bag here. A nice hen, two liddle d-duck off'n the mere, and a gurt buck rabbit I shoulda left a two-month yet. Meat's meat. Shall you and your lady sleep over, master?'

'The barn suits,' Piers said.

It needed another two hours for Davy's stew to be ready, and it could have done with three more, but they were too hungry to complain. That night they spent in the barn warm in the straw and clasped together. Isabella slept deeply, but Piers had much to think about and to plan. He was thankful that his father and Harry were from home, otherwise there would have been a hue and cry about the forest by now. He worried about the women left to make nightmares for themselves, and about Richard, to whom he could not explain. Hearing Davy move at first light, Piers left Isabella sleeping and went out of doors.

'Look'ee, Davy,' he said, putting his arm confidentially

about the man's shoulders and speaking in a low voice.
'I need you to ride fast to Ghylls Hatch. You must speak
to none but my brother Richard, and see you tell him to
come fast to me here. And you must tell him to search in
my chest for the little bag of coin that's there, and bring it.'
'I'll go when?' asked Davy.
'Now. Well—after you eat a bite.'
'Now's best,' said Davy.
Piers watched him ride off on his cheerful, disreputable
nag. The morning was very clear and fine and promising.
Isabella came from the barn and paused beside him and
took his hand. She stood in the growing sunlight, as still
as truth.
'That were a good night's rest you got, my love,' he said.
'When I woke I remembered. I need not lie. Like a
gift, it was.'
'No more fears, then.'
'I made a good confession,' she said, smiling at him.
'It was you shrived me, husband—no priest could do
better. Last evening I feared you and I feared God. I
am shriven of both those sins.'
Again the awfulness of his responsibilities sat upon
Piers like a great load. Here in the sunshine, on the
threshold of a new way of life, she might think herself
steadfast. But her life had run so strangely he wondered
if it could ever be re-made. Perhaps there would always
be a mystery in her that he could not touch . . .
When Richard came to Tillow Holt, he stamped and
shouted.
'Why? Why come you set out, Piers? What o' my
godson? How'll I ever see'm now? When'll you come
home?'
'I'll come,' Piers said.
'When? When?'
'Somewhen—I can't say. Only tell my father this:
The mystery is solved. Tell him that. He'll know.'
'But is it days or years?' Richard insisted, near to
crying.

'I don't know, minnow. I can't say. But one day I dessay you'll find me down the pool, fishing like we always done.'

Richard stood with his shoulders hunched up and his misery made Piers curse and shout at him.

'Get home and stop your snivelling. Come you're a man, you'll know right enough. You'll know.'

Richard got up on Breeze and rode off without another word, and that made Piers run after, calling to him. 'Take care, Dickory. Look after yourself. Maybe it won't be long—'

'To hell!' shouted Richard, and galloped off.

Since it was summertime, living was not difficult. As they moved east, they found the hay still in the cutting. Later there would be the harvest, later still the hops. At such times all labour was welcome, and the movement of so many about the countryside from farm to farm saved a man on the road from any fear of being taken up for vagrancy. Between haysel and harvest, Piers took work at a furnace; halfway into Kent, he called it, and there he learnt a harder toil than any that had come his way before. Here all was well ordered, the master keeping his men and their families in two rows of cottages he had built for the purpose. In this way he could keep the men longer, though the cottages, little more than hovels, were even so forever changing hands. Either an itinerant worker could not stand the hardship of the trade and moved on after a short time, or else the work itself, the hot and the cold, took its own toll and despatched its victims in their earlier years. But there were some old men who had survived, either at furnace or forge, and were wise in their craft and puffed up with their own survival. They were set to gentler tasks—tallying, checking timber, dealing with the charcoal burners who were a race apart, almost with a language of their own. Perhaps, Piers thought, he was learning all this for Harry. In this employment he grew lean, harder, older, even in a few weeks.

They left the iron mill when it was harvest time, moving further across country where there were larger farms, needing more workers. By this time Isabella had only a few more weeks to wait for the birth of Richard's godson. She was well and contented, a harvest in herself, and so Piers was contented, too. The long summer days were filled with hard work for him, work that he knew well enough from all the summers since he was six years old and went with Harry to help the gleaners. He had always been content at such times, but now it went much deeper. He was no longer the master's son, but a servant. This was the simplest life he had ever lived, and whatever came next he would not forget it. He lived hard, earning bread for himself and his wife, sleeping in straw and rising at cockcrow to a day always longer than the last. He missed no one at this time, not even his father, not even his grandmother, not even the horses he loved to care for. He knew that he was living from day to day, he had no knowledge of where it could all lead, but for the time what he had was enough.

The farmer Piers called Master was a decent man, a freeholder, modest, good to his workers, treating them as his fellows and always kindly anxious for the well-being of their families. When the harvest was home he spoke to Piers of further employment—they spoke the same tongue for he had come into Kent from further west.

'There's little I can give—having all my own men and none more needed this time o' year. But my sister, over Maidstone way, she's likely in a different case. Seeing she bin widowed years past, she'm her own master. She grow timber and there's pritnear always felling and such, and the scutchett and that to be cleared. She'll think kindly of a Sussex man. So go her way, and ask for Widow Pilgrove, and say who t'were sent thee.'

'I'm grateful, master,' said Piers.

'What's more, the way things go with your wife, a

woman for gaffer's not to be sneezed on. My sister niver
had her own but she's rarely tender wi' young things.
Come she'll take you that'll be a suent place.'

Again Piers thanked him, this time from a full heart.
Taking each day as it came, he had so far fended off his
worries about the birth. Once the child was born it
might not be so easy to get a living, the season advancing
and better shelter needed. The Widow Pilgrove sounded
to be the best person he could hope to find at this time.
He would be glad, too, to move within reach of a town,
for he wanted news of how the world was going. With
the coming and going from market town to market town
in the common way of trade, he might get word of Lewes
and of the doings of Master Robin Halacre, the agent of
the Crown by reason of being the Earl of Essex's man.
Men came and went quickly in such positions, even Piers
knew that. If he could learn that Robin was fallen from
favour it could be his solution. He had not spoken once
about returning home since the morning they left Tillow
Holt, for he loved Isabella's present tranquillity and could
not bear to risk seeing her eyes cloud with fear again.

The weather stayed so fine that the drive across the
country was a holiday. On all sides the harvest was home,
the fields stripped and tidy, the stacks built and thatched.
The land lay quiet briefly enough—the ploughs would
be out in another week or two, and they were praying for
rain in all the village churches, for the ground was hard
as marble. Piers whistled as he drove his horse, and
Isabella sang quietly to herself. He was uneasy to consider
that they had no clothes for the baby when it should be
born, and he wondered that she seemed to have no care
in the matter. He had a little money now, so they would
go together to the market and buy what was needed.
He thought soberly that she might not know what to
buy, for she had only known Anne's baby and the story
of one at the beginning of Christian time. She might be
hard pressed to choose between lace caps and swaddling
bands. He looked sideways at her as they drove, and now

he laughed to himself; for he might almost as well have married the changeling bride of the legend.

They were bound for a village called East Forstal, which turned out to be still a good many miles from Maidstone. They reached the place on a Sunday morning and the church bells ceased ringing as they drove along the village street.

'We are in time,' said Isabella.

Piers was glad, as she was, for it made a good start in a new place. They went into the church and pushed their way in at the back among some stares and whispering. Up by the rood screen, in a place of comfort—she had a chair and a cushion to kneel on—a woman of thirty or so made her devotions with enthusiasm. This was surely the Widow Pilgrove herself. When the blessing had been given and the congregation trooped out, everyone waited until she had passed. She was a fine-looking woman with black hair, a high complexion and a firm, confident face. Piers gave her time to get home, and then they went to the farm. Behind it stretched acres of woodland, but the farm itself was handsome, too, with many good barns and a solid clean house with windows set in sturdy mullions.

A girl was pumping water outside the kitchen door.

'I've a message for Widow Pilgrove,' Piers told her, 'that come from her brother Funnell.'

The girl looked pertly at Piers and then rather slyly at Isabella. She went indoors without a word, but she returned very shortly with her mistress—who was rolling back her sleeves as she came, the fine churchgoer turning back neatly into a farmer.

'Peg tell me you come from my brother.'

'Aye, madam,' Piers said. 'He say you could be wanting labour for timber.'

'Tell me his name, then,' she said.

'It were Farmer Funnell, over by Horsmonden—at harvest time.'

'God bless him!' she cried. 'I miss him. Was it a good

year for him? I wish he might prosper. But you never come out o' Kent, surelye? That's my home tongue you speak.' She looked him up and down in a considering but friendly manner, and then glanced at Isabella. 'Well, I do need men. You look pretty spry and strong. Too, I see your wife need a roof pretty soon. Aye, pretty soon, I reckon.'

'She do so, madam,' Piers said.

'I'll try how you work. Peg—take and show 'em where they can bide. Old Jacob's place. He die last week,' she explained, 'rest his dear soul.' Before Piers could thank her she began to turn back into the house. Then she paused at the doorsill. 'And pray do as I tell all the rest,' she said in her firm clear voice. 'I am not madam to you, but master. Let that be plain.'

Though there was at present no felling, last year's culling and coppicing had to be worked over, cut into lengths, in some cases stripped of bark, or otherwise treated. Widow Pilgrove contracted to supply wood surprisingly far afield, even as far as Maidstone, where she had a brother-in-law always ready to put her in the way of business. So there was much chopping of logs and faggots. The chips and the dust—the scutchett, as it was called by both Piers and his 'master'—had to be gathered thriftily into baskets, and this went for firing indoors. All this was moderately hard work, but it was pleasant, and the scent of the wood on his hands in some way gave Piers pleasure. It was another craft he learned daily.

'One day I'll find some body or other to teach me masonry,' he told Isabella. 'Well—it's the way not to starve, and I never did reckon much of soft hands.'

She smiled but said nothing. These days she was very quiet, waiting and listening in a manner that left him often very lonely. He knew that women were bound to be strange at such times—even bouncing Anne had grown somewhat remote. He was anxious, yet anxiety was not the sum of his sensations. In some strange way, he was jealous, too. He saw her calm as he had longed for her to be, more than merely tranquil as in the earlier summer days when he knew he had done right in bringing her away. The calm was too much. It was a threat to their life together though he could not know why he felt this so certainly. When the child was born he would have to hold her fast or even now she might elude him. He had a rival, and that rival was her conscience.

Whatever else, they could not have found a better place than this with Widow Pilgrove. Her brother had spoken truly of her care for young things. One of the girls, Betsy, who worked in the kitchen, had given birth to twin boys a few days before Piers and Isabella came to the farm, and one of the babies had died. It seemed as if Widow Pilgrove mourned the loss far more than the young mother, who had no husband, but would never be turned away from her place here.

'I give my girls the clothes I once set aside for my own,' the widow told Piers and Isabella. 'A great coffer of them I had.' She laughed, not bitterly, but a little mocking of her own unrealised hopes. 'And naun to show for it but one stillbirth! Then my good man died and took my children with him.'

'Did you never think to marry again—master?' Piers asked.

'I never saw his match,' she answered. Then she turned to the silent Isabella. 'Come in with me now, my dear, and we'll choose what you'd best have. If there's too little left by now—well, weaver comes here in a week or two and we'll think about cloth.' She took Isabella's hand, it was cold and she began to chafe it between her own. 'Not long now, surelye,' she said.

It was in that same week that an order for three waggonloads of wood came from the town, with something more than a request that it be delivered urgently. Piers and two others loaded up, and then the three of them must take the waggons on the road to Maidstone.

148

The order came at a bad time. For two days past Isabella had been restless, and it was clear enough that the baby would soon be born. He set off with the others in the early hours of a misty morning, distressed at the thought that the birth might take place while he was away. The Widow Pilgrove laughed at him, and said his work in the matter was done long ago, and it was for the women to get on with the rest. He was touched to see that she was in a rather bustling mood, excited by the prospect of the infant. And calling her *Master* as he set out with the rest, he found it hard not to laugh in her face, though it would have been a very gentle laugh.

No sun came to clear the mist that autumn day, and the sky was dirty. The weather was breaking at last, the rain not far away. Because he was worried, Piers now felt very far from home, and all the way to the town he thought not only of Isabella but of Ghylls Hatch and what might be happening there, and he longed with all his heart to be back safely at home among his own people. The still dank mist oppressed him. It opened and closed to let them through, the waggons enormously loaded, the big-footed horses straining and slipping on the hills, the men toiling on foot beside them; Piers, the man they called Old Slattery and a lean-necked lad named Tom Tanner.

They came to the town in the late afternoon, the place was bustling and noisy. Old Slattery was the leading waggoner, and he went in search of his instructions. There was a trough under the pump in the market place where they had drawn up, and Piers and Tom let the horses drink two by two. Presently Old Slattery returned, and with him a rotund little man, bald-headed and somewhat consequential, who said they should unload and stack there where they stood. Having given his orders loudly, he strutted away.

'Here?' Piers said. 'Here where we stand? Ask me, that's a dunch way to keep a wood pile.'

Old Slattery gave him an odd look. 'I should'a know'd

why the hurry. Master never guessed, that's sure—so you and Tom, keep mum.'

Piers frowned. 'What'll we be mum about?'

'Well—one money bag's as good as the next,' the older man said. 'Still—I'd sooner what I chop fetched up on honest hearths.'

Lanky Tom Tanner looked from Slattery to Piers and swallowed hard.

'I can't think of only one reason for faggots in a market place—'

'Get to unloading and shut your gab,' grunted Slattery.

They worked in silence, while a small crowd gathered to watch them. An elderly man with a schoolmasterly look stood near to Piers and after a bit spoke to him, asking only at first where he was from.

'That's no task for a lad of your stamp,' he said presently.

'I can labour good as the next,' Piers answered shortly. His oppression now was so great he had difficulty in breathing evenly as he slung and stacked the wood.

'You've not the face that builds pyres,' the man insisted. 'Don't you know of the fine pack of heretics in the gaol here? All to be tried and executed.'

'If they're to be tried—' Piers began.

'You can't have an execution without a trial—that's good sense. But the end's the same. A heretic's condemned out of his own mouth and must burn. They're so stubborn they seldom take back any word they've spoken. And if they do recant—they must still be burnt for their own souls' sake.'

Piers wiped the sweat off his face and straightened his back, but he dared not look the man in the eye. He saw the wood neatly piling, Old Slattery and Tom working away doggedly, and he clenched his teeth in case he vomited.

'What men are they?' he asked.

'Men of flesh and blood, like all the rest of us. Some brought here from Rochester or Canterbury—they're easier tried in batches. There's some newly great man being sent to see it done—next week or somewhen.'

'Who's he?'

'There's half a dozen, they say, working through the south country. Simons, Bennett . . . Some such names. Halacre, Brown . . . I can't tell which.'

'Robin Halacre,' Piers said.

'You know more of him than I do . . .'

At this point Slattery yelled at Piers to get on with the job, for he and Tom were unloaded, and there was time for a pint or so before starting back. Piers tumbled out the last of his load, slapped up the tail of the waggon and went after the other two into the tavern. He looked over his shoulder as he went, but his schoolmaster, or whoever he might be, had gone on his way.

Over the ale there was much talk about the trial and those who stood to be condemned. Though Old Slattery had grimaced at first to discover what the wood was for, he now enjoyed the modest importance it gave him. One townsman, happy to display his own particular knowledge, said there were ten or twelve heretics in all.

'As well you bring a good load in!' he said, giving a great guffaw, and nudging Old Slattery so hard that he almost went sprawling off the bench. 'Stoke up and burn the lot, I say. Two on 'em's monks. There's one in a habit and one right out of the cloister wears cloak and doublet to make out he's good as any man. It's more likely treason than heresy they'll charge him with. But the end's the same. The other brother used to be at the great Priory at Lewes—I had that from the gatekeeper.'

'Who's to make judgment?' Piers asked, wanting to strike him, but speaking quietly enough.

'The King's own best man, my friend. A great and noble scourge of heretics and traitors, so they say. A great seeker after truth. One Master Halacre.'

'Halacre?' cried Slattery, slopping his ale in excitement. 'What, old Ben Halacre? Old Ben?'

This caused such an uproar of merriment that for a

time no one could answer him for thigh slapping and bellows of ungovernable mirth.

'Ben's eighty if he's a day,' the man explained to Piers, 'and bin in these parts since a lad. I doubt he ever heard of heretics. He's a clothier by trade. No, no!' he cried, butting Old Slattery again. 'It's some other—they're a tribe here and westward—calling cousins, maybe. But tradesmen and craftsmen—not men to try their fellows, or move grandly.'

Piers and Tom Tanner had difficulty in dragging Old Slattery from this excellent company and setting him on the road for home. It was already dusk when they set out, and all along the way he was shouting for them to stop at the roadside inns. Piers cursed the delay. Everything about the day had thrown a burden on his mind, and he tried vainly to fix his thoughts on birth and hope. All seemed weary and spent, the year moving to its close, the day ended and the sky heavy.

As they rode into the yard at last, the girl Betsy came from the kitchen, smiling all over her silly, pretty face.

'Come in, you!' she shouted to Piers. 'You got away the right day—but come you in now, and quick about it. All's done and your wife has summat to show.'

Piers stood like a fool, unsure whether he should break into laughter or tears.

'It's your daughter, friend! After all that carrying and hard work—naun but a poor female child come of it in the end!'

11

Who Lie in Gaol . . .

For several days Piers was so greatly moved by the state of parenthood that he thought of nothing else. The baby seemed healthy, and they would call her Catherine, after his own mother. Isabella had said this should be so. When he returned that night and went striding indoors, he had found her looking flushed and beautiful, more like any other woman than he had seen her since the early days of their marriage. He felt triumphant, positive, and home seemed suddenly near at hand. Within twenty-four hours the vision was fading. She had grown pale, languid, remote and almost as silent as in the days when they called her his stranger.

'I do fear for her,' he said at last to Widow Pilgrove.

'She's weary. She's ended a long hard task. It's a sore shame that men may not bring forth now and then!' cried Widow Pilgrove. She looked at him rather searchingly, as he had known her do before now. 'But she is in truth a delicate dainty creature,' she said. 'No wife for a labouring man, I'd say. If she be so.'

'We are safely wed,' Piers answered.

'That was not my meaning, as I think you know. But you labour well enough for me, as you done for my brother. So be that's how you choose to live, I've no cause to be picksome.'

That night or the next, when the baby cried to be fed, Piers lay awake. Isabella fed the child and sat rocking her for some time; then she lay down once more and all was quiet. It was some time after midnight, a light frost was at the window, and in the deep quiet Piers knew that Isabella, too, was wakeful. Then, later, he heard her crying and felt how the bed shook as she sobbed.

'Wife?' he said gently. 'What ails you?'

She gave a most terrible, rending cry: 'I am damned! I am damned!' and burst into loud wild tears that frightened him so much he felt completely helpless. There was such despair in her voice that he felt as if the frost had come in under the roof and settled on his heart. 'I have damned us all!' she cried. 'I have broken my vow and I shall not be forgiven! And nor shall you. And nor shall this poor child we have made between us—in great sin!'

Piers tried then to take her in his arms, as much for his comfort as for hers, but she pulled away as if his touch burnt her.

'You said you were content, Isabella. You trusted in God and in me to care for you. Nothing has changed. We are ourselves as we were then. I never felt but that we should be blessed and you made me think you felt so, too.'

'We cheated!'

He did not answer. Perhaps it was true. *If you have the courage to wed a mystery* . . . The memory of his father made him groan, he so longed for his counsel. He needed help most bitterly and had cut himself off from those who might have given it—his grandmother, perhaps most of all—while death had taken Dom Thomas, his other most certain guide. There was no one at hand whom he could turn to . . .

Then he remembered.

In the morning Piers went to his master and asked her indulgence. He needed to return to Maidstone where, he said, he had on the day the wood was carted heard of an old friend in distress. 'I wanted naun that day but to get home and find my wife safe delivered. But now I'm niggled by the thought of him.'

'What's his trouble?' she asked. 'It must be sore if you're to spend a day of my time seeking him.'

'It's the sorest trouble a man can know, master. He's nigh to death.'

'Well, then—go if you must, and God save his soul, poor creature. But no maundering by the way, mind—and never say a woman for gaffer's too soft to be respected.'

'I never will,' Piers said.

'Your wife's lower than I like to see,' she said. 'She and the babe had best come in by the kitchen fire, come you're from home. Betsy and Peg and I shall try to cheer her. This day or next, the weaver should be calling. We'll all choose cloth for Christmas gowns.'

'God keep you, master,' he said warmly.

He set out on the heavy old horse that had drawn the cart for them all the way from Ghylls Hatch. It was hardly a riding animal but he had not felt able to push his good fortune by asking to borrow a better. The day was dull again, the frost had broken into damp and the countryside was still as a picture painted on a church wall. As he neared the town he began to feel an unpleasant chill at the thought of what he was undertaking. If he was to be admitted to see the monk from St Pancras he must first beard Robin Halacre. That was task enough. But if Robin had not yet arrived for the hearings, then the journey would probably have been in vain; he could only talk himself into the prison, he had not enough money to bribe his way in.

When he reached the town, Piers made his way to the fine cluster of buildings by the river in which his drinking companion of the last visit had told him prisoners might be housed. He dismounted and tied up his horse, giving a groat to a lad to keep an eye on him. Close by was the archbishop's palace, this being a manor of the See of Canterbury. Also a range of buildings with an ecclesiastical air, with some windows smashed and the lead partly stripped from the roof; but there was a good deal of coming and going about the better part of this building. Piers looked about him hopefully, as if he expected to see a familiar face; the schoolmasterly man he had spoken to, perhaps, when the wood was unloading. Eventually he stopped a fine tall young fellow with a cheerful face, and asked his help.

'Aye—they're held over yonder,' he said, when Piers had asked his questions. 'The trial's tomorrow noon. And the next noon, they say'll be the burning. So if you want a good place, best be early.'

That he might not appear to know too much, Piers asked was the King come.

'Hardly that, friend! This is not Westminster or York. But his man is here, three days now, and seems fine enough.'

'Is it Master Halacre!' Piers asked.

'Some such . . . Nay, for sure, it's Halacre and nothing less.'

'How shall I speak with him? And where?'

After the months of working and wandering about the countryside, Piers looked no finer than any other labouring man.

'*Where* is yonder by the old college. But *how*?' The young man looked him up and down and laughed. '*How's* your own bother.'

Piers went towards the building the young man had pointed out and was stopped at the entry by some guard or porter.

'Master Halacre, if you please,' Piers said, for there seemed nothing to lose by boldness.

'If I please, or if you please?'

'Both,' Piers agreed. 'But I pray you—tell Master

Halacre that his old friend Piers Medley is here to speak
with him.'

The man said nothing, but continued to eye Piers
thoughtfully; for though he looked like a servant he
spoke like a master. There was a great struggle in the
man's mind, which should win, and his eyes showed the
two considerations shuttling back and fore. At last he
shouted for someone to take a message. It seemed a long
wait, and Piers grew chillier as the minutes went on. But
he would have staked a good deal on Robin's curiosity
getting the better of him.

Since their last meeting at the Easter fair, Robin had
changed quite remarkably. He had aged, he had put on
weight, his clothes were impressive and he had become
very grand in manner. He sat in a great chair behind a
splendid table, with a couple of secretaries and a servant
or two hovering and attentive. He was writing when Piers
entered, and without looking up he waved him to a
stool—then kept him waiting like one accused until he
had finished a sentence of such elaboration that it seemed
likely to cover more than its page.

Then he said, 'Ah—Piers.'

Powerful he might have become, and dangerous; but
to any who had known him in his boyhood he seemed
ridiculous, too. Wisely or not, Piers relaxed, and he
could not quite stifle a laugh as he answered, 'Ah—Robin.'

Robin sanded the paper and blew it carefully. Then he
handed it to one of his secretaries to fold and waved him
away; and his fellow, and the servants also. He smiled
tolerantly as he did so. He had adopted an altogether
different manner—lofty but a little jovial, confirmed in
his achievement, perhaps.

'You have come a long way to torment me, Piers
Medley,' he said as the door closed.

'I was hereabouts. Chance.'

'Well, I do not forget my friends, and you know it.

I wish I might say the same of you. I asked for your help
in the matter of the Leethwaite woman and you left me
in the dark to make my own way.'

'I am careful of my grandmother,' Piers said. 'I did
not care to disturb her.'

'I doubt any of us could disturb Dame Cecily,' Robin
said amiably. 'She re-makes the law for her own use.
She does not know the smell of danger. On the whole, I
admire her for it.'

'She would be grateful,' Piers said humbly.

Robin seemed to give Piers his full attention for the
first time. 'In God's name—what's come to you? You
look like anybody's hind. Have you fallen on ill times?
I heard you were from home.'

'Aye,' Piers said easily, 'Harry's set to work the iron
on our land. I came into Kent to see how men proceed in
these parts. There's always new ways in such matters.
But the manner to learn 'em is with your own two hands.
That I've done. And to some purpose.' These half lies
slid easily off Piers's tongue, and he went on quickly,
before Robin could regain the initiative. 'But, Robin, I
come to you for a different purpose, that's clear. You
know well there's a man waiting to be examined who was
of the community at St Pancras. For my uncle's sake—
let me see him.'

'There you go,' Robin burst out, 'with your monkish
friends again! Can't you learn what's good for you, Piers
Medley?'

'He'll die, they say. So then I'll have one monkish
friend the less.'

'And soon none, I trust. For those who won't conform
must go. Happily many save trouble by leaving the
country.' He frowned at Piers. 'Well—they say a condemned man can gain a favour.'

'Condemned?'

'Enough's been heard. But the people like to know
justice has been done.'

'Robin—for your own soul's sake—let me speak to him.'

'And what of your soul?' Robin said piously. 'Should I not also think of that? If I loose you to a heretic's rantings—how shall I stand in the matter should you fall?'

A few months ago, had he spoken so, he would have had a fanatical fire in his eye. His manner was most subtly changed. It had about it now a smoothness, a sophistication that suggested he had attained his goal and knew well how to maintain himself in a desired capacity. In spite of the nature of his work, its dealings in life and death and doctrine, he seemed to Piers to bear the stamp of a favoured schoolboy praised by his masters. When he said *And what of your soul?* his voice was tinged, if not with cynicism, at least with irony.

'It's not much I ask,' Piers insisted. 'And I can hardly believe I have to supplicate a fellow like you—I still remember how you slit your hose top to hem falling out an apple tree!'

Robin laughed, then. A fat sound, Piers found it, but let no distaste show in his face.

'Well—if he choose to speak with you—then let him. But see you're not corrupted. It's as much treason as heresy he'll die for. He's obdurate as Lucifer about the Pope; he speaks great evil of the King.' He picked up and tinkled a little silver bell and at once a secretary came running. 'Write me a prison pass,' Robin said, 'and do it now. And spare your thanks,' he told Piers, as his secretary sat down to the task. 'It's pleasant to be able to humour an old schoolfellow. And since I shall not be in these parts for some long time to come—I'll leave you to remember me kindly, with all previous transgressions quite over-looked.'

'Where shall you go?' Piers asked, afraid to hope too much.

'You shall be the first to wish me well, Piers. The news was waiting for me when I reached here. With one thing and another there are offices to be filled. I am to have a Deanery.' He looked at Piers and smiled. 'You see why

you find me in a generous mood? Of course I have first
to be confirmed in Holy Orders. But in these days happily
things move fast enough for even the most impatient—
the most zealous of men.'

Piers had never been inside a prison before. His father
had told him of once visiting a man held in the Tower.
He had spoken of the cold, and it was the cold that struck
now at Piers, taking him between the shoulder blades and
behind the knees. He would have been glad to turn and
run away, but he had come for a purpose and he would
try to achieve it, for it might mean the balance between
contentment and despair. He took with him into the
heavy dark place his own troubles and Isabella's.

Until the very moment when he ducked his head under
the lintel and heard the door swung and locked behind
him, Piers had half expected to find himself facing
Brother Francis or Brother Hilary. But the thin, ravaged
man in his torn and stained habit was Dom Stephen, who
had at one time been Sub-Prior. Piers had never known
him except by sight and through hearing his uncle speak
of him.

'Who's there?' he asked, peering at the visitor. He had
been sitting on a heap of straw with his back against the
wall and he struggled to his feet. He straightened his
shabby gown and made some attempt to stand upright;
but he was not a young man and things had not gone well
for him. 'More questions?' he asked.

'Father—I am Piers Medley. Dom Thomas of your
community was my uncle.'

'Is it possible—?'

'My uncle is dead, God rest his soul.'

'Amen. He was a good man. There are not many of us
left from St Pancras, I daresay.' He looked at Piers and
frowned a little. 'I cannot tell how to greet you, my son—
as a fellow prisoner? As some instrument of authority?'

'As neither, father. As a supplicant. I heard how it was

with you, and I need counsel. And I have come some way
to seek it.'

'It is surely sought in strange places!' Dom Stephen
said, and he laughed a little. 'Have they not told you I am
both heretic and traitor? I will not deny the authority of
the Pope, I will not accept the religious authority of the
King. It is the same thing, but they make two charges of
it. I shall be burnt with the rest. Do you know that?'

'Aye, father,' Piers said, mumbling it, sick at heart.

'And it is certain you are not some agent sent to trip
me and make my case still blacker?'

'I have told you who I am. I know you as a priest of
Holy Church. I need your judgment, and maybe your
absolution. But first you must tell me if indeed I've
sinned. And you must answer me a question: Since a
man and wife are one flesh, may they be one conscience?
And if you may absolve a fault shared—may not the
absolution, too, be shared? So that if I leave here shriven,
shall she, too, be free?'

'You have a fine philosophical way of argument, to be
sure,' the monk said, and again he laughed gently. 'If I
were at any other part of my life than its end, my mind
might be too clouded for me to accept the proposition.
But say what you have come to say and I shall answer
you as best I may. I am too near the face of God at this
moment to deal in anything but truth as it now seems
to me.' He pulled his cowl up over his head and sat down
stiffly on the three-legged stool that was all the furniture
in the place. 'Kneel down, my child,' he said, 'and have
no fear. This shall be a confessional for both of us.'

Then Piers, in a low and hurried voice, for he feared
he might be called out of the cell before he concluded,
told his tale. He told of going to the Priory at his uncle's
call, of taking the great brass tablet into hiding, of the
meeting at the church gate; then the death of Dom
Thomas, his own acceptance of the charge his uncle laid
upon him, the journey home. He told how Isabella had
grown well but stayed silent, and how she had become

one of them at Ghylls Hatch, and still he had fought his feeling for her. He spoke of their marriage. As the hardest part of the tale came near, he began to stammer a little, but it had to come. He told Dom Stephen what Isabella had told him, on the day that Kate Leethwaite was taken from her husband and carried away.

'So then, father, I could only think of losing her. I soothed her and she seemed calm. We came away into this different countryside. Last week our daughter was born.'

He paused there. His grief and disappointment came over him so strongly and sadly that it was not that he prayed behind his hands but that he struggled not to weep.

Dom Stephen was silent, too, waiting. 'And next?' he said at last.

'It is all to do again! Though she was a novice merely, and that by her father's choosing, she cannot forget her vow that was not absolved when she was thrown back on the world. All that has passed between us now seems to her to spell damnation.'

'And how does it seem to you, my son?'

'It seems to me she has fallen into the sin of despair, father. But as I kneel here I wonder if I expect too much of Heaven—and my sin is the sin of presumption.'

'How are we any of us to understand?' the monk said quietly and slowly. 'We talk of faith and charity, but it is hope that sustains me now. Hope is most modest of all—and so it shall be for you never to deny hope, and so it should be for her. Tell her this. In a few hours, perhaps, I may see my Maker face to face. I shall not forget you. So, also, tell her that. And, Piers Medley, I accept your philosophy of one conscience, though it may all be called part of my heresy, and I give you both absolution. And my blessing, which is likely the last I shall give, so I thank you for asking it. Go in simplicity. Peace be with you both.'

Piers had been kneeling sternly upright on the stone

floor and the chill had crept through his whole body. But as he sank back on his heels and took his hands from his face, he felt as if he, too, had long been a prisoner, and that now his chains had been struck off.

'Pray for me,' Dom Stephen said, as Piers rose at last to his feet. 'And do not pity me. I have no place in this world now. I shall feel nothing—nothing but the joy of my release.'

At first Piers rode very soberly on his way home, but gradually his own life became more urgent to him than another man's death and he was filled with impatience at the miles to be covered. It had begun to rain, and this, added to the dreadful chill he had brought from the prison, was enough to keep him shivering as if he rode in midwinter. He tried to stir up his horse, but though the creature was as always willing enough, it was simply not capable of much. So it was dark by several hours by the time he reached home.

No one was about, and there was only one dog loose when he rode in, though the rest set up a clamour at the sound of the hoofs. He saw to his horse and then crossed the yard to what would long be called Jacob's Croft from its last occupier. He pushed the latch and went in to darkness. The draught from the opening door blew a few red eyes into life on the hearth and a mouse scuttled. Otherwise all was silence and he felt a snatch of anxiety. Then he remembered that Widow Pilgrove had said she would keep Isabella and the babe by her own fireside until he returned.

Piers knelt on the hearth and raked up the ashes. Fed with kindlings the fire soon looked comfortable. The iron pot was standing on the trivet. He looked in and smelt the contents hungrily, then set the pot to hang above the fire. It seemed a long time since he had tasted food and he began to look forward to the meal. After, when all was settled and warm, he would tell Isabella of the day's encounters. He thought how he would ease away her fears. How they would be able to start living again.

Without wasting any more time, he left his own fire and went across to the farmhouse to fetch her home.

Peg opened the door to him, and the big kitchen fire made his own efforts look meagre. Betsy was sitting in the firelight, her baby kicking on her lap.

'Is the Master indoors, Peg?'

'Inside. In the parlour.'

'I'm come for Isabella and the baby.'

'Bella's home, long since.'

'No,' he said.

'For sure she is,' Betsy put in. 'The weaver come, and Master was all for Isabella choosing cloth—like she give us all a gown for Christmas.'

'And did she not, then?'

'She run off,' Peg said, 'Didn' she run off, Bet?'

'She's a most timmersome thing,' Betsy said. ' "Shy as a woodmouse," Master call her.'

'She's not at home,' Piers repeated. 'The fire was good as out.'

'She took faint, maybe, and goo off to bed. She do seem a little poorly.'

'Yes,' he said. 'O'course she done that.'

He ran back across the yard and along the side of the big barn and came again to his own doorway. There was a little loft above that just took the bed, and there was a slant of horn in the roof that gave some light, though not much in this dark night. He took the ladder three rungs at a time, calling as he went, stumbled on the top rung and fell into the room. It was utterly dark, but he knew at once that the bed was cold and empty; as the room was, and all the walls and space above and below it, and the night beyond.

12

The Bitter End

As he went pelting back to the house Piers was shouting for help without knowing it. The dogs broke into barking again and a child somewhere cried out in fear as it was waked from sleep by the noise. Peg flung open the kitchen door, and two of the farm men came running after Piers, calling out to know what was wrong. So that there was a crowd of them at the kitchen door when Widow Pilgrove swept into the room and banged her palm on the table for quiet.

'What's the pother?' she demanded. 'Decent working bodies should be a-bed.'

'My wife, master,' Piers cried, 'and the babe, also . . . There's none at home—empty . . .'

'I tell him she went home long ago,' Betsy said, moving into the circle. 'You remember, master—when the weaver come.'

'That's true what Betsy say,' said Peg. 'She run off, and I never did see why. I call out to her—Weaver's here, I call—and then I went to fetch you, master. When I get back she were gone. I see the tail of her running across the yard.'

'She'll not be far,' Widow Pilgrove said. 'Set on to make a search, John. You, too, Martin. You and Piers get about it. Three's enough, so you keep cool heads. You stir up the fire, Peg, and get warm covers. Now, Piers—lift your chin a bit jaunty. You look like you picked her up dead a'ready. She'll not be far in the time, I tell you. She only give birth a few days gone—and there's the baby to cart along. It's not sense that she'd get far.' Then she changed her reassuring tone and cried to him sharp and harsh as flints—'Wake up, man! It's a foul enough night for a bitch with pups, let alone her.'

It was raining steadily by now; though not heavily yet with a quiet persistence that soon plastered the hair on their heads and made runnels into their eyes. John took command, sending Martin one way, Piers another, saying 'I'll see to the granary and the mill. Whosoever comes on her, give a halloo. Take a lantern, Piers.'

Piers stood holding the lantern helplessly. He did not know how to start looking, most of all because he feared what he might find. Then Martin gave him a shove and pulled him along a bit. After that, as if he had been started down a long hill where he was bound to gather momentum, Piers moved fast. He went into the row of barns, one after the other, calling. When silence answered him he began to ransack each building in turn, tearing at straw and hay, kicking aside bundles and pulling up traps that led into cold stores dug out of the chilly ground. He leapt up into the lofts and scoured those, tossing everything he could lay hands on to one side, everything that might conceal a woman and child. Yet all the time it seemed to him futile. Why should she hide? What should have sent her suddenly into flight? It was not what she would do—not what she needed to do, even if she were entirely hounded by her own tormented spirit. But if that, why had it suddenly driven her? And what course must it lead her to? He thought in dread of the nearby

river, but put that hard away from him. Women at these
times after childbirth could get very low in spirit, he knew
that, and her circumstances were particularly dangerous
. . . He could not and dared not answer his own
questions. The effort of his violent searching was making
him sweat and pant, and he kept groaning as he went
from place to place and there was nothing. Then he began
to search over the ground, seeking something she might
have dropped as she went. So that he left the farm
buildings and quartered the yard and all the ground about
it, like a hound seeking its scent and becoming all the
more frantic at not finding it. He returned in desperation
to the chaffy quiet of well-kept barns, the warm stink of
byres, the milky smell of the dairy that most of all filled
him with anguish, for it made him think of the baby's
milk-smeared mouth as drowsiness took it in the midst
of feeding.

At last, defeated, he went back to the house. Martin
was there already, and John came almost at the same time
as empty-handed as the others.

Now Widow Pilgrove was pacing about, frowning and
biting her lip.

'What would she fear?' she demanded, when Piers
came in. 'Had you two differed? Had she been frightened
by aught you did? For if so—may God forgive you, you
have driven her out! If we do not find her soon she will
die. Betsy—think again. Peg, was there nothing said
between you that might send her running? Think, girl!'

'Why, what could there be?' Peg said, beginning to cry.
'I saw the weaver coming and called out to her—Here be
weaver, or some such. And she went out the door before
I knew. Then he was there, and you walked in, and it
were all of an hour before we finished looking and
choosing.'

'I do remember you said she'd surely be back—that
she'd gone outside,' Widow Pilgrove said. 'Now you,
Betsy. Was it all as Peg says, think you? Nothing more?'

'I can't think other. There I sat by the fire, and Peg at

the window watching for weaver, and Bella was by me, wi' the baby in her arms. Then Peg call out: Here come Dobbin Halacre across the yard—'

'Ah, no!' Piers cried. 'No!'

'That's the weaver,' Widow Pilgrove said. 'Dobbin's old Ben's nephew . . . Tom's brother—Hester's grandson . . . There's a plenty of 'em—you know that, surelye? Come out of Sussex—mostly weavers and such.'

'Not all,' Piers said; and he felt they might almost as well give up and go to their beds. With that supposed threat at her back she could run till she dropped. 'Of all names given to men,' he said, 'that one she most fear. Halacre!' He put his two hands over his ears as if he would shut out the sounds of men, and rocked himself in a near-frenzy to think of the sourness of it—the silly trick played by chance. The rest watched him silently, then glanced at one another uneasily, and shrugged and frowned.

'Mull some ale, Peg,' Widow Pilgrove said then. 'John, get Will and Ned here, and rouse up any other you can trust. First we'll warm our bodies—though God knows we may not warm our hearts—then all set out again. And if we search all night through till morning, we must find her.'

When morning came, they were still searching, plodding now in weariness and gloom. The rain had stopped. The lanterns had long burnt out. First light laid a glimmer along the horizon, touched the highest sky and died again momentarily. Then the glimmer steadied and with infinite effort the day slowly began in a leaden sky. Men were bound to stop searching and begin their work, for the beasts depending on them, on which they in turn depended, were ordered by time, not circumstance, and what they had to give must be taken when it was ready.

Piers knew he had to begin the day's work like any other. He was down at the riverside when the first light began, forcing himself to accept the dreariest possibility of all. But there was no sign for him there, either, and he trudged up across the meadows to where the farm, lying at one end of the village, made an almost identical pair with the church farm stretching behind and alongside the graveyard. Very dark, barely seen for the elms about it and the scarcely paler sky, the church itself stood squat and square as it had done for upward of four hundred years. And immediately he was aware of the place, Piers knew what he should never have forgotten—that Isabella would come here, as she had fled into the mere outline of the church at Mantlemass, instinctively seeking sanctuary.

If he had kept his wits, he must have known where he would find her now.

He shoved at the heavy door, pitted with age and worm, and it creaked as it let him in. The interior of the church was as black as a cave, and even the lamp burning at the altar was no more than a spark on the gloom. He stood listening, finding it difficult to call out in a place he knew to be hallowed—to shout in the presence of God. Hardly breathing, he bent his head to catch the least sound— and almost immediately he did hear something. It could have been no more than a rat, but it sounded far more like a shoe, shifted a bare fraction on the gritty flags of the chancel floor. He did call out then—'Isabella!' The sound sped like a bird round the walls and spiralled up into the belfry.

He heard her running and he blundered after her through the darkness, calling as he went, 'It is I—Piers! Wait!' and praying for light; though he knew that even when it came it could not be more than a glimmer here. He began to blunder into the pillars, and all the time he could hear her darting from place to place, could hear her breathing, and once even felt her skirts brush by. She must be out of her mind with fear to run so. How could he force some understanding on her unless he caught and held her and spoke close by her ear. It was as if she heard only the pursuit, not the sound of his voice, not the calling, increasingly desperate, of her name. And though once he heard her fall and gasp, she was up and away again in no time at all, as far from him as ever; and as he lunged towards the place where she had seemed to stumble, he crashed against the door to the rood loft, that was standing open, and half stunned himself. He had to close his eyes and clutch at the carved screen until his head stopped swimming.

When he opened his eyes it seemed suddenly lighter— or at least the utter denseness of the dark was pierced by a faint glimmering that displayed the shapes of the windows. And at once he saw something—a movement, the movement of a shadow, and he darted forward. That time he had his hand on her and grabbed at her sleeve, but to his horror she screamed and dragged away so hard that the sleeve was torn from his fingers. There was a quick flurry of movement, then a creaking. He was almost sure she had fled up the wooden steps into the belfry. If so, he had her cornered.

At the base of the tower the utter dark began again, but when he looked up he saw the grey light just touching the wooden slats of the bell tower, and the mass of the two bells hanging silently side by side, yet for all that looking as if they would break into clamour at a touch. He did think for a wild moment of pulling on the rope and so summoning help—but she was so close beneath the clappers he knew he dare not. He went up after her, not fast but steadily, speaking to her as he went, soothing, cajoling, laughing, even, in his desire to calm her.

The steps ended in a small platform, and there was a thin rope stretched from corner to corner, that could be grabbed if need be. It was still too dark to see Isabella's face, and so she would not see his. He put out a hand towards her. 'My dear one,' he called her. 'My love. My dearest wife . . . Isabella . . .' Then he had his fingers at her wrist and needed only one more effort to grasp her.

At the touch, Isabella screamed again and again, and hurled herself back from him. Her foot went over the edge of the platform, and she grabbed at the rope, but it was old and snapped and she was gone. He did not see her falling through the dark. He only heard the ground receive her, and the silence that followed.

He had difficulty in getting back down the steps, because he went too fast and slipped and barely saved himself from following her. The light was now a little more and he saw where she was lying. He fell on his knees beside her, longing for more light, praying for it, desperate to see her face whatever it might tell him. She moved very slightly and moaned and instantly his heart leapt. But after that she was still.

Just then the door creaked open, and the parish priest, a very old man, came limping in to set about the first mass of the day. He was too poor-sighted to notice them there, but he let in enough light for Piers to see Isabella's face and to know beyond any help in the world that he had lost her.

Then he heard the baby crying from another part of the church . . .

It took Piers a long time to ride back across Kent and so to the forest and the moment when he could know that nothing but a mile or so separated him from home. He could have made better time, for he had exchanged his cart and the old horse for a better animal. But he went in company with his thoughts and they kept him too much occupied to kick up any decent speed.

First there had been much bitterness with the old priest, who insisted that she had taken her own life and therefore should not be buried in consecrated ground. Piers had fought him and cursed him, but day by day the old man refused to be shaken. He would have buried her at the crossroads with a stake through her heart, if he dared—so Widow Pilgrove said. His age, she said, had

not helped him to tolerate the events of the past few
years. Piers had wished him dead, and wished it aloud
and with such malice that later he was ashamed. In the
end, the old priest grudgingly allowed Isabella just inside
the churchyard wall; Widow Pilgrove had said she would
see the spot planted with a rose tree later on, and that, she
told him, should be a fair and a fine monument.

Then Piers had struggled with them all to take his own
child in his arms and ride home with her. Here he had his
Master to fight, and she was his master indeed. 'Take her
if you will, and kill her, too. Only a brute would do it.'
He said stupidly that he had raised a new born foal before
now, that had lost its mother's milk. He would wrap the
child warmly and bind it to his body under his cloak and
he would ride home in two days. With goats' milk and
cloth to soak it up he would keep his daughter suckled as
he had kept Sola, his most cherished mare. 'Take her,
then,' Widow Pilgrove said again. 'What's it to me if you
kill her? She's no child of mine.' Betsy had fostered the
child since she was carried home from the cold church,
and it she who made him see reason in the end. 'Look how
I brought two into the world, and lost one on 'em. For
why other than to have another give me? So leave her till
she's safe grown, for poor Bella's sake.'

With all this heavy on him Piers made slow progress
indeed, and it was all of a month from the day Isabella
died to the day he found himself on home ground again.
He picked his way through the forest and the sight of it
lifted his spirits for the first time, for here at least was
something left unchanged. He was half tempted to go
straight to Mantlemass, then later to Ghylls Hatch, but
he feared to startle his grandmother too much by suddenly
walking in. She was growing old, though her fine spirit
made this hard to accept—he did not want to harm her
by any sudden shock. He made his way instead down to
the fishing pool, halfway between one house and the
other. He dismounted and let the horse drink long and
thirstily. The quiet by the pool was the quiet he had

known since childhood. He had come here bewildered when his mother died. He was something more than twenty years old now and it all seemed a long time ago.

The day was bright and still, the trees still half golden, the high pale sky without any whiff of cloud, yet touched with the coming of winter. The water ran as usual, even the boulders that it chinked over were the same; and in the shadow of the bank, where it overhung a sudden deep pocket of bright brown stones, he saw a trout lazing, head into the current, utterly still, as if concerned only with the protection of its own shadow. There was a redbreast singing as there always seemed to be in this place. That made him think of another Robin, the simple student from a country home, who had seemed to see a new freedom but found in it only the means to take freedom from others. It seemed very strange indeed to think of Robin Halacre, the son and grandson of weavers, making his way among the great, seizing what advantages offered and never mind too much about conscience—what sort of a cleric would he make, Dean Halacre, of wherever it might be? No doubt he would come within the orbit of the King himself. Piers did not often think about the King, but now it came to him that if there had been no divorced Queen Katherine, no quarrel with the Pope because of it, there might have been no closure of the religious houses, no dispossessed monks, no half-released nuns; no Isabella. And so by declension, no foresty child waiting for him in Kent.

At first Piers sat by the pool with his head in his hands. Then gradually he began to feel his taut muscles unknotting, his nerves that were stretched tight by unhappiness, loosening a little; the stillness like a hidden hand stroked and eased them. He lay back against the bank and put his hands, then, behind his head, his face into the sun, his eyes closed. A leaf or two sailed to the surface of the water and spun away downstream, and the trout flicked his tail and was still again. The feeling that filled Piers then could not be contentment, but it was acceptance; of all the past time of struggling, first against what he must have known by instinct was a doomed love, then the fight to keep it living in the face of bitter circumstance. He thought of the happiness of their marriage in its early days, when he had felt like a powerful enchanter, and the peaceful time when they were alone before their daughter was born. The more he thought of it, the more he knew that the mystery had remained. And all this, with the shock and horror of her death, seethed itself in the curious cauldron called experience, making him twice what he had been, while by some paradox it took half of him away. He understood this only in part, knowing merely at that time how much of life could be left to him, knowing even more keenly that he did not want to lose it. In the first hideous moments of despair he had been ready to throw what was left away. But what was left was less his life than another's. His own flesh and blood had cried out for help and he had been bound to answer.

After a time, almost sleeping, Piers knew he was no longer alone. He opened his eyes cautiously. Richard was standing a few yards away.

Richard said nothing and nor did Piers. The boy came nearer and sat down beside his brother on the bank, watching him sideways, as if he might dart away as the trout had done when Richard's shadow touched the water. The two of them sat in silence and stillness for what seemed a long time. When Piers spoke at last he only said, 'I'm home.'

'Alone,' said Richard.

'Alone. She could as well have been the Queen of Fairyland after all, minnow. She was not for me.'

'She's dead. Isabella's dead?'

'A month or so ago. I've lost the time a little.' Then seeing how troubled the boy looked, he added, 'But I have your godchild safe—though in another place.'

'A girl again,' Richard said, even at this moment sounding not too resigned, 'else you'd surelye say my *godson*.'

'Catherine Medley. Half an orphan. Lovingly fostered, I promise.'

Again they were silent, and then Richard said, 'I come here near every day. You said to find you here.'

'I did.'

'Once when I come, my father was by the water. He was weeping, Piers.'

'Not angry . . .'

'Never angry. I give him your message—about the mystery solved. He blamed himself, he said then.'

'He should not . . . Oh, I'll be glad to see him!'

'It's been a sad time,' said Richard, in his wise-old-man voice. He put his hand almost timidly on Piers's arm. 'When'll we fetch her home?'

'Soon as maybe.'

'And I'll go with you.'

'Aye, minnow. She'll need you, that I'm sure.'

'So now first I'll fetch you home, Piers,' Richard said.

He got to his feet and stood waiting, his shoulders up because he was both nervous and excited, sad and merry. Piers rose with some difficulty, for he had ridden far and there was no joy in his bones, only the great sighing relief of homecoming. He whistled to the horse, which pricked its ears and began to follow. Piers put his arm across Richard's shoulders, which eased at once, and Richard held him round the waist to help him. They went up the steep bank together in the direction of home; as they had so often done in the days before sad strange Isabella came to change their lives.